sex education

sex education

JANNI VISMAN

BLOOMSBURY

First published in Great Britain 2002
This paperback edition published 2003

Copyright © 2002 by Janni Visman

Grateful acknowledgement is made to the following for
permission to reprint previously published material:

Biology A Functional Approach by M. B. V. Roberts
© M. B. V. Roberts 1971, 1976, 1982, 1986, Nelson Thornes Ltd,
Thomas Nelson and Sons Ltd

'That's the Way (I Like It)' Words and Music by
Harry W Casey and Richard Finch © 1975,
Reproduced by permission of EMI Longitude Music, USA
Reproduced by permission of EMI Music Publishing Ltd,
London WC2H 0QY

'Get Down Tonight' Words and Music by
Harry W Casey and Richard Finch © 1974
EMI Music Publishing Inc, USA
Peermusic (UK) Ltd, 8–14 Verulam Street, London, WC1X 8LX

'Golden Years' Words and Music by David Bowie © 1976,
EMI Music Publishing Ltd/Moth Music/Tintoretto Music/Chrysalis Music Ltd
Tintoretto Music administered by RZP Music Inc for the
USA and Canada and by RZO Music Ltd for the World excluding
the USA and Canada

The moral right of the author has been asserted

Bloomsbury Publishing Plc, 38 Soho Square, London W1D 3HB

A CIP catalogue record is available from the British Library

ISBN 07475 6156 7

10 9 8 7 6 5 4 3 2 1

Typeset by Hewer Text Ltd, Edinburgh
Printed in Great Britain by Clays Ltd, St Ives plc

acknowledgements

For their helpfulness and support, I am grateful to
the following: Barbara Creed, Christina Dunhill,
Phil Gray, Vicky Jung, Stacy Marking,
Marian McCarthy, Laura Morris, Alexandra Pringle,
Susannah Rickards, and Miles Visman. Thanks also
to all friends and family for their encouragement.

for elke

Gabriel is kneeling on his right knee. He holds a white lily in his left hand and his right hand is outstretched to Mary. Mary is standing near a lectern that holds her open book. She holds both her arms out towards Gabriel. Beyond them the view from the window is as it has always been. Immediately outside, the tall delicate ash tree, behind it the curve of the river, a boat and a bridge, on either side green fields, and at the back on the left the castle with its spires on the hill. Everything looks quiet and serene.

Everything is how it should be. Every fold of Gabriel's pink robe, the half-close of his pale yellow wings, the hold of Mary's hands, the placement of each of her fingers in the air, how their eyes look to each other's raised hands. His intently, hers shyly.

Her eyes look to his hand; his eyes look to her hand. I still can't tell if she is moving towards him or pulling away from him. If she is reaching out to touch his hand and meet his body for the first time or if they have just separated for the last time and, with her eyes cast down to his hand, she moves away. There is a tenderness between them, a concern in their eyes, a softness of expression as if trying to understand the moment and each other.

His eyes look to her hand; her eyes look to his hand. Everything in the picture focuses the viewer's eye to the space between their hands. All the desire and pain between them is caught there.

I notice for the first time that the forefinger of Gabriel's hand rests on the same plane as the edge of the window, as if he has pushed the wall aside to make the window and reveal the world beyond. Behind him is the distant view; behind her is only the dark grey wall of her room. He offers her the world, offers to take her from her books and solitude. If she touches his hand she will go outside. And the way she stands she looks unsteady as if she is just about to fall at his feet. The bend of her knee as it collapses beneath her blue gown catches the light.

part one

selina and me

the pink thing

It is a hot summer day. Selina and I are kneeling side by side in her garden. Our baby dolls are naked, belly down on our laps. We are spanking them hard for wetting their nappies. Scattered around us are all the accoutrements of infantile motherhood. Milk bottles with candy-pink teats, hair-brushes adorned with butterflies, a bath full with water, prams, pastel-coloured baby clothes and nappies.

Selina picks up her doll by the ankles. She lifts it to shoulder height and starts to smack it again. Long shoulder-to-wrist smacks that make the doll bounce.

'This is what they do when real babies are born,' she says, 'to make them breathe, Mummy told me.'

She turns the doll the right way round and cradles it in her arms. 'Don't cry,' she says softly, stroking the doll's hair. 'Don't cry.'

My doll is down on her new nappy and I fold each point to meet under her belly button, securing it with a safety pin.

'Selina, we'll have real babies one day, real ones that talk.'

I lean forward to get a milk bottle, bring it to the doll's petulant little lips. 'Don't cry,' I say.

'We can't have babies until we have bosoms and hair down there,' she says. Selina always knows everything. She points between her legs and then she starts to sing. 'Go to sleep, go to sleep, you're my very own baby.' As she rocks

5

her doll its eyes blink open and shut. 'Close your eyes,' she says.

We are only wearing our matching bikini bottoms. I look down at my flat chest, poke my nipples, bring my doll's mouth to one of them.

'To close her eyes you have to lay her down; she has to be still,' I say.

Selina reluctantly puts down the doll. Its eyes close. Selina also closes her eyes. She does this when she's angry, or when I am right and she is wrong.

'There is no milk in you,' she says as she opens her eyes.

I pull the doll away from my nipple.

'I bet you don't know how real babies are made,' she says.

The news disturbs me. I think babies are not made, they are had, they are always there inside the mother, waiting to be born. I shake my head and then lie on my side holding my doll tight against my stomach. I know this much: that the baby lives inside the tummy. The doll is very warm from being in the sun. It smells like pear drops.

Selina has lain down close behind me, her knees inside my knees. She speaks into my hair, her voice low to show me it is a secret.

'Mummy says to make real babies, the daddy, well, he puts his pink thing inside a hole in the mummy and wiggles it around and tickles her.'

I scan my father's naked body in my mind for something pink. I find nothing. I scan my mother's body for holes. There are plenty: her mouth, her nose, her ears.

I turn to face Selina. 'What's a pink thing?' I ask.

She grabs my wrist and gives me a Chinese burn. 'Promise you won't tell anyone what I told you.'

6

'I promise – what's a pink thing?'

Selina stands up. She holds her doll by its hair, little bits of blonde poke out of the top of her fist. She starts to swing the doll so its eyes blink madly.

'If you don't know then you're a silly, a silly, a silly.'

It is the worst thing in the world to be a silly. Selina stands up and dances around me in circles, her doll dangling at her side. She dances wider and wider until she is skirting the perimeter of the garden. I get up and, clutching my doll under my arm, scoop together my things and dawdle towards the gap in the garden fence that takes me home. I give her one final beseeching look before going through the gap. She is busy singing to her doll: *Maddy is a silly. Maddy is a silly. Maddy is a silly . . .*

The next day I ask Selina a hundred times what the pink thing is but she won't say, she just shakes her brown curls, closes her brown eyes and makes a little kissing mouth. I get so angry with her I push her over, but she still won't tell me. She just lies in the grass on her back kicking her legs.

'I bet you don't even know what it is,' I say. This just makes her laugh more.

The question continues to trouble me, but I pretend I don't care and I don't ask her any more.

Some weeks later I'm in the kitchen; it's after supper; my mother is washing dishes, my father drying. I am sitting at the table making cards full of princesses for Selina, writing 'I love you' and 'Be my friend for ever and ever' in the corners.

My mother's laughing makes me look up. My father has his arms around her waist and he is sticking out his tongue. It's pink. The revelation is like someone clapping their hands very loud in my head; it resounds throughout my body, sends a shiver down my spine. 'It's his tongue,' I say to myself. 'It's his tongue that is the pink thing.' I sit bolt upright and watch. He wiggles his tongue around, then he lunges and his tongue is now in my mother's ear. She can't stop laughing, tries to catch her breath in short inward gasps that make her whole body heave. Only when she screams does he relent and pull away. Her ear is full of spit, but they are both laughing and smiling. She kisses him on the mouth and then they look at me. I am spellbound; they start to laugh again.

My parent's bedroom is next to mine. That night I am woken by the sound of my mother's heavy breathing; I know my father is sticking his tongue in her ear again.

That my father had to do it again was not a problem for me. Selina had said babies only came on certain magic days and mummies and daddies had to try each day to catch one.

I lay there in my bed and I imagined the tiny weeny baby floating down my mother's ear. It floated into her mind and then fell slowly slowly inside her body until it came to rest in her belly.

The next day I told Selina I had found out what the pink thing was. I stuck out my tongue and held the tip of it between my finger and thumb. She put her thinking face on. Whenever she thinks hard her face seems to fold inwards to a V and a vertical line appears between her eyebrows. 'I know,' she said, 'but you can't do this, can you?' She put out her tongue and curled it upwards so that it touched her nose.

'And the hole?' she asked when she had finished showing off.

'The ear,' I said proudly. I took hold of my ears and pulled them forward, so that they stuck out, to prove my point. She wanted to know which one.

'The right one, of course.'

'Just testing,' she said.

I knew she didn't know about either the tongue or the ear. I pretended she did. She knew I knew; she was extra nice to me all day. Did all the things I asked her to do. Let me choose what games to play. Let me boss her around. Even admitted that I was taller than her.

Nine months later my sister is born. On the telly there are wars in Vietnam and Ireland. There are riots in Paris. There are plans for a man to go to the moon.

We stand back to back. She slides her hand over the top of her head, makes little chopping motions to the back of my skull.

9

danger danger shark shark

Selina and me are wearing our matching plimsolls. Hers are blue and mine are green. We run and skip along the walls that line each front garden in our street, jump the small gaps between them or scale the cast-iron gates. At number 16 there is no wall. Instead there is an old beech tree, so big that it hides the house behind it. We help each other up to the lower branch and climb to the fork in the trunk. From here we count the sharks. There are always well over a hundred circling the ground beneath the tree, their fins ripping through the concrete and paving slabs. Sometimes they show us their mean mouths filled with shining sharp teeth that they snap at us. There are sharks all along the street but by the tree is their favourite place.

Earlier, I was nearly eaten. I lost my footing tripping over my lace. I lay on the ground, flailing with my arms to beat the beasts away, and screamed out 'I'm dying', as are the rules. Selina immediately said the magic words: 'Danger Danger Shark Shark.' Saying it over and over as she lay down on her stomach and reached out to touch my raised hand. She touched me before my fifth 'I'm dying' and I was saved. One more time and I would have been completely eaten up. I would have been deaded. In all the time we have played this game we have always saved each other. We have never died. After she touched me I got up and she pulled me back on to the wall and we carried on.

Getting down from the branch on the other side of the

tree to the wall below is the hardest part of the game. The top of the wall is four feet from the ground. The branch is six feet from the ground and only just reaches the wall. We lower ourselves so we are hanging from the branch by our hands. We swing hand over hand like monkeys to the end of the branch and then turn ourselves so our backs are to the wall. From here it is possible to get a foothold. Slowly, you have to walk the wall backwards, one foot behind the other, and then let go of the branch quickly bringing your arms up and out to keep your balance. I am much better at this than Selina, which annoys her. Although she is always ahead of me on the walls, at the tree I always go first so if she loses balance I am already on the wall to save her. Today, Jayne, the new girl from round the corner, comes to play the game with us. When we get to the tree, Selina says, 'This is really really hard – so I'll go first to show you how to do it.' All the time she says this she glares at me which tells me not to say anything. Today, there are even more sharks than usual swimming in our pavement sea, to impress and scare the new girl. Selina tells her there are more than a thousand.

Selina's hands are on the branch, her feet are on the wall. I cannot see her because my back is to the wall but I hear the soles of her feet move against the grit of the brick. Then I feel the branch judder as she releases her grip. And then I hear the loud thump as she hits the ground. I call out: 'Danger Danger Shark Shark!' And again I call it out: 'Danger Danger Shark Shark!'

'I'm dying . . .' calls Selina. She is lying on her back, arching her neck, looking in pain.

'Danger Danger Shark Shark!'

'I'm dying . . .'

12

I am still hanging on the branch. I see her raising her hands towards me. I swing my legs out.

'Maddy – I'm dying – quick,' she shouts. 'My legs, they've eaten my legs!'

She only has to say it two more times and she will be dead. I walk backwards and let go. My heart is beating so fast that I think it is going to explode in my chest. I can hear its thump thump thump in my ears. I have to hold my arms out longer than I like to stay upright. The air against my body is heavy, seems to be pushing off, but I keep my balance.

'I'm dying – ooh, it hurts so much.' Selina says this in a pathetic way, in a way that says my not being there to save her is the deepest betrayal in the world.

I am on my stomach.

'I'm coming, Selina, I'm coming.'

I reach out my hand and my fingers are an inch from her fingers, but before I can touch her she gives one final scream and says, 'I'm dying . . .' She lets her voice trail to a whisper and slowly lowers her arm to the ground. I feel as if my stomach is full of rocks, as if the brick wall I lie on had gone through my skin, has filled my insides. I break out in a cold sweat. I can hardly speak, my mouth is so dry.

'Selina, Selina – I'm sorry. Selina, please wake up now.'

Selina just lies there motionless. I jump down from the wall and shake her. She is like a rag doll. Her body goes wherever I push it but she herself does not move or open her eyes. I lift one of her eyelids; still there is no response. I feel sick.

'Selina – please, please wake up.' I am kneeling by her by now. Jayne has scrambled down the tree and stands quietly beside me. We both look down at her.

13

'Shout in her ear,' says Jayne, kneeling down beside me. I bend close to her and yell. 'S-E-L-I-N-A!'

There is not even the slightest twitch. I can feel my heart breaking inside me leaving a huge sense of hollowness. For what seems like for ever I stare at her. She stays motionless. I turn and hit Jayne hard across the face and burst into tears.

On hearing my first sob, Selina lifts her hand and finds my hair and tugs at it.

'Gotcha,' she says. 'Gotcha.'

Outside, time seems to stand still. Freeze. Inside, the joy I feel starts at my heart and moves out like a star. I cannot find enough space in my body for it. I can see the three of us from above. Selina propped up on her elbows now. Laughing. Me and Jayne kneeling beside her. Me hitting her. Not hard, on the upper arm. Me kissing her. I'm thinking, Selina can do anything. Anything. As long as she doesn't die. And then I'm there. My eyes full of Selina's face. Her warm cheek against my lips as I kiss her again.

Jayne wants to kiss her as well. She says so, and leans forward. I won't let her. I guard Selina's face with my hands.

'Go away!'

Selina is still laughing and singing 'Gotcha'. She stops. 'Yes, go away, skinny.'

Jayne won't go. I have to get up. Stamp my foot. Chase her away halfway down the street.

She is shouting, 'I hate you, Maddy.'

I am shouting, 'I don't care.'

I help Selina up and we walk home with our arms slung over each other's shoulders. She is still pleased that she tricked me. She has that look on her face that she does when she has won a game. Sort of tight around the cheeks like she is smiling although she isn't. I make her promise she won't die again. She says it was my fault that she died but she still promises. We clinch our deal; she crooks her little finger and I crook mine. We link them and shake them. We sing the lines:

Make up
Make up
Never do it again.

I make her do it twice to be sure.

Later, I try to draw the joy I felt that Selina was not dead. I want it to be something I can wear. It starts off as a ring. It ends up as a necklace with a huge red stone that is smooth and shiny and soft and spiky all at the same time.

I cut the necklace out and gave it to Selina. To protect her. She wore it for a day. She wore it in the bath and it disintegrated. I didn't care. It made her bathwater bright red and stained her skin for days like she had sunburn. I liked this. I liked that she had taken my joy skin-deep.

the anatomy book

We have been given a book – the sort of book in which each page is layered. If you pull tags, sections lift away to reveal what is underneath. It is like a paper autopsy of the human body. A full page is taken up with a naked woman's form cut off at the neck and top of her legs. On the opposite side is the equivalent male version. I pull the first tag on the woman's body and her skin moves away from her belly. A crude shape that resembles the outline of a goat's head with horns is exposed. Two small oval shapes float by the tip of each horn.

Selina reads the words out, pointing to each bit. 'Ovaries, fallopian tubes, womb.' She taps her fingers on the oval shapes again. 'These are ovaries; they're full of eggs.'

At first I think Selina says aviaries. This makes sense because birds lay eggs. She says 'fallopian tubes' so it sounds like 'fall open tubes'.

I pull a tag on the man. I think: no womb, vagina becomes penis, ovaries outside the body.

'Inside-out woman,' I say to Selina.

'Sssh. This is the vagina,' she says, pointing to a small road that goes up between the lady's legs. I see that it gets narrower at the bottom of the goat's chin.

'I can read,' I say.

'This is where the man puts his penis.'

She shows me, laying a finger across it. She makes little sliding movements with it so it goes higher into the woman.

She slides her finger across the page to the picture of the penis and rubs it up and down.

I've seen my father's as he walks around naked in the morning. I never thought it was for baby-making; it was for going to the toilet. I'm glad I don't have one. They look like they don't belong to the body. They look unfinished. They just seem to dangle there and flop about. I touched Selina's brother Gary's once, behind the big tree at the back of their parents' garden. I smoothed the very tip of it with my forefinger. When I touched it suddenly grew bigger. It felt like the surface of a mushroom. Cold and damp. I ran away. The one in the picture looks different. More grown-up. Selina is still rubbing her finger up and down it.

'I've touched a real one,' I tell her.

'So have I,' she says. I know she is lying. I would know if she had. Selina tells me everything.

Selina now taps at where the vagina road gets very narrow in the picture.

'This is a very tiny gap,' she says.

The name of it is the cervix.

Selina reads from the book. 'Once a month an egg is released from one of the ovaries and makes its way down the fallopian tubes . . .' Selina points to the goat's horns. 'While it is doing this the womb prepares itself for the baby . . .'

I tell her again that I can read. She tells me to shut up.

The womb is the goat's face. I outline it with my finger. It is self-contained; it doesn't go to the ear. I am disappointed. Selina smacks my hand away to continue reading.

'One of the millions of sperm from the man's penis fertilises the egg in the fallopian tube. The egg starts dividing into more and more cells. As it does it moves down towards the womb, plants itself into the lining of the womb and grows into a baby.'

I continue reading over her in a louder voice but she just gets louder still.

'If no fertilisation takes place the egg disintegrates and the lining of the womb falls away. This is called menstruation and shows itself as blood coming out of the vagina.'

We fall into each other's hair in fits of giggles.

Every month my mother says she is bleeding like a stuck pig, only when she was pregnant with my sister she didn't say it. She told me she bled from the tummy, but that was all. I have seen all the things she uses to catch the blood. They are kept in the toilet in a special wooden box.

Selina and I are both just twelve. Our nipples have started to swell. There is hair growing under our arms and between our legs. We have been warned about the monthly blood. The book is a gift to both of us from our mothers.

We turn the page and pull all the tags. All the things Selina has just described are illustrated one by one with a final picture of a baby curled up in the mother's womb, its little hands together as if in prayer.

My favourite part of the sequence is the cloud of sperm as it fills the vagina. There are millions of them, painted in silver so they are all glittery and shiny. There is something noble about the idea of all these millions of things fighting over one egg, like knights on horseback fighting for the damsel in the tower.

'You'll break it,' says Selina, as I pull on the tag for the sixth time.

'There's millions of them, millions and millions and millions,' I say.

We put down the book, lie down on the floor and take off our pants. We investigate our own bodies.

'It feels like the inside of my mouth,' Selina says.

'Yes,' I say, 'but without teeth.'

I pull my finger out and bring it up to my nose. It smells like the seaside so I lick it. It doesn't taste of the sea. It tastes like the very weak lemon water my mother drinks in the mornings.

I whisper this to Selina in the dark. She says I'm disgusting because I licked my finger. Then I hear her lick hers. She doesn't like me doing anything before her. She tells me her finger tastes of peppermint. She will have babies that taste of peppermints. I will have babies that taste of lemons. I think, my babies may be sour, but at least nobody will want to eat them. Very quietly, so Selina won't notice, I put my finger in my ear and then taste it. It is equally bitter.

magic words

Mr Douglas has a voice that sounds as if he is talking through cotton wool. Low and soft, so the class has to be quiet to listen. He is completely bald. His head is always shiny. Mr Douglas says today he is going to explain to us how the Virgin Mary became with child. He has a visual aid. He always has visual aids. Last week he showed us a painting of the Madonna and child. This week he is going to tell us how she came to be with child but was still a Virgin. Because we were confused: everyone knows mothers can't be Virgins.

Selina looks smug. She thinks she knows it all now because of the pop-up book. She says science is better than religion. More true. Her mother said so. I told her I liked the idea of being a Virgin mother. No boys. No penises like damp mushrooms. Just the baby already inside the woman. Ready-made. Waiting to be brought to life. She closed her eyes and told me to be quiet.

Mr Douglas uncurls the picture against his chest. He opens it to the span of his outstretched arms. '*The Annunciation*,' he says as it is fully revealed. He holds it up so everyone can see.

It is a painting of an angel and a woman. They are inside a room. The angel is kneeling, the woman is standing, her hands stretched out in front of her towards him. She looks scared. The angel looks sad and lost. In the background, there is a window. In the landscape, a tree, a river and green fields, and in the distance, castles on hills.

He secures the picture to the wall with drawing pins. He says the angel is Gabriel and the woman is Mary. He points to them.

Selina wants to know why they aren't undressed. Gabriel and Mary. She asks me and then asks him. 'Why aren't they naked?'

The classroom fills with giggles.

'They should be naked if they're going to have sex.'

'They are not going to have sex. Gabriel is telling Mary she is the chosen one,' he says.

Selina takes a deep breath. 'My mum says they all say that, men to women, when they want it.'

I tell her to shut up. This is important.

Mr Douglas puts his finger to his lips. The class quietens. He resumes.

'The painting is called *The Annunciation* because Gabriel is announcing to Mary she is going to be with child and then she became with child. Simple as that.'

'No sex?' I ask.

'No sex,' Mr Douglas confirms.

Selina shakes her head. She looks disgusted. Mr Douglas slaps his Bible and tells everyone to turn to the appropriate page. I don't bother. I have heard all I need to hear. I know all I need to know. I nudge Selina.

'See.'

'What?'

'I was right.'

I steal the picture of the Annunciation. I go back during break and take it down off the board. I stick it to the wall opposite my bed, next to my map of the world. I make Selina promise she won't tell on me. If she does I will tell the teachers she made me do it. I tell her to tell my mum that we were all given one but that she lost hers. Selina says she thinks I am turning into a loony.

She doesn't see what I see. How the Annunciation proves that a tongue in the ear gives life to the child that is waiting inside. In the Annunciation it is words, but words can't be made without a tongue, so there is no difference between tongues and words. They are the same. It is the soul of the baby that floats down the mother's ear. Sex is only the half of it. Sex only wakes the child up. Makes it ready to receive its soul.

Gabriel whispered into Mary's ear. She became with child. It was magic.

Selina is staring at me staring at the picture. She whispers that she thinks Gabriel isn't as handsome as David Cassidy. I think he looks beautiful: long blond curls and blue eyes. He looks kind and gentle. Understanding. He also looks a bit lonely.

The painting is by Botticelli. It has been reproduced courtesy of the Uffizi Gallery in Florence. It says so in tiny letters in the bottom right-hand corner. I run a piece of red cotton from the edge of the picture to where Florence is in Italy, like they do in geography to show where things come from. Secure the cotton at both ends with pins. Kiss Gabriel.

gabriel

Gabriel has long blond curls and blue eyes. Gabriel is sweet, kind and gentle. Gabriel is understanding. Gabriel is lonely.

He stands as I walk into the room. He waits for me to speak.

I pose the questions like I have seen in the agony aunt pages of the teenage mags Selina and I buy.

Dear Gabriel,
  My best friend Selina keeps telling the boys I fancy that I fancy them. Then she gets off with them. Why does she do this?

Gabriel is always wise. He speaks softly and slowly. 'Selina is very insecure and needs to reassured by everyone, especially the boys, that she is loved and needed. Selina is also very jealous of you because you have straight blonde hair that is fashionable and parts easily in the middle.'

Whenever I have a problem, especially with Selina, I go and see Gabriel.

Sometimes when we can't solve the problem Gabriel and I go for a walk along the river banks, up the hill to the castle and beyond, where there is a path that leads into a forest.

If the problem is very bad I walk quietly, my arms folded, eyes to ground. Gabriel himself says very little but smiles a lot and, from time to time, points out various birds and animals. Eagle, squirrel, magpie, fox, jay. The path twists and turns; around us the trees grow thick, thin out, grow thick again.

At the darkest part of the forest there is always a breeze that makes all the branches creak like a hundred old doors being opened. We wait for it. Hear it gathering pace as it comes towards us, captures us, our hair blown across our faces, Gabriel's wings ruffled. And then it passes through beyond us, fades out into quietness, a few old twigs falling into the undergrowth.

Gabriel takes my hand. 'Close your eyes,' he says, and I close my eyes, but continue walking, led by him. I know to stay silent. Each time we come here he does this.

In the darkness, my every sensation becomes more pronounced. The touch of his skin against mine and the breeze against my face, the sound of each footstep, the papery flap of a bird's wing, the buzz of an insect, the hush of the moving leaves in the wind. The whole world seems to rush in and fill my blood with the promise of good things.

I always want this moment to last for ever. I once whispered this desire to him, my eyes still closed. He very gently squeezed my hand. 'Sssh . . . you will spoil it,' he said. And he is right, because each time I go beyond being in the moment and try to capture it, it vanishes and everything is ordinary again, or rather I'm back again. Me filling me, instead of the world filling me. I want the world filling me – making 'me' empty, making me feel like I am floating, filling me to the skin with nothing and everything. Making 'me' vanish.

If I disturb the moment Gabriel makes me stand still a while, eyes tightly closed. He focuses me on a bird call, a magpie's caw or the mew of an eagle to get me back. He knows when I am there again, says that my hand grows

26

suddenly warmer to the touch. Then he leads me on again in the dark.

When he tells me to open my eyes we walk in silence, but eagerly, towards the pool of sun at the end of the path where the trees open out into a clearing. There are tall yellow flowers growing here, and a small pond, long grass, a lone apple tree. Here we lie and sunbathe for a while. Gabriel has to lie on his stomach on account of his wings, which he keeps high and tight together so that the sun can get to his shoulders. Everything feels peaceful and calm.

'So are you happy now, Maddy?' he says.

'I think so.'

'So we can go home.'

We take the long route back, crossing the bridge to the other side of the river bank, walking through the fields, not saying very much. He kisses me on the forehead and I say goodbye at his front door and we resume our positions. Him kneeling. Me on the bed being called down to supper.

girls and boys

threading the needle

The grey skirt is straight and loose and falls to mid-calf, the blazer a black box with sleeves that hang halfway down the hand, the shirt an undefined mass of white.

In our school uniforms we look like rectangles with small heads and feet. We watch ourselves in the shop-window reflections as we walk to school. We hate the way we look.

We wear bras now and mini-briefs that ride up into the crack of our bottoms. We have curves that go in and out. We have tits and arses. We want to show them off. We don't want to be disguised as rectangles. We want to be the women we now are.

It takes one weekend to customise our uniforms. I do it at my house. I set the sewing machine up in front of the telly; I get the scissors, the chalk and the pins. Selina stands on the table watching the telly and I move round her, pinning each item to fit, telling her to keep still.

I am good at sewing. I always have been. It comes naturally, easily. My mother says I sewed my first button on when I was three. 'Very carefully on to the corner of a white sheet,' she points out to Selina. Selina can't even thread a needle without pricking herself. It was me that used to make all the clothes for our dolls. Hers in blue, mine in green. My mother also reminds her of this.

I pin Selina's skirt to mid-thigh. The other skirts I pencil tight down the hip to the knee. Next I dart the shirts at the bust and stream them to fit our waists, narrow the arms and move the buttons down so they will reveal cleavage. The blazers I make into jackets. I fit them with shoulder pads and heighten the sleeves to expose the wrist.

We watch ourselves in all the mirrors and all the shop windows. Our curves are mapped. We are women now. We walk tall and proud and talk and laugh very loudly. Louder still when we buy our new platform-wedged shoes. Our hands always running through our hair when we get it cut with flick-backs. We can't stop smiling because the bus conductor doesn't believe that we should only pay half.

Selina and me, we are the bee's knees at school. We look the business. The teachers can't tell us off. It's not as if we aren't still wearing the uniform. It's only when we wear our pencil skirts that they can have a go because the skirts make us late for school and then for lessons. Our tiny steps make our bums and shoulders wiggle.

The older girls stare at us enviously from a distance. They don't have to wear uniforms but we know we look better than they do. The other girls in our year gather round us in a small circle and admire us, plucking at the hems and seams. Selina knows I will be asked to do the same for others. She makes me promise I won't do it for anyone else.

'Not even Jayne?' I say.

'Not even Jayne,' she says.

I must just do it for her and myself.

'Promise,' she says.

'Promise,' I say, and we wiggle together across the play-ground, arms folded, through the boys playing football and penny-up. Some of them call out, 'Titselina.' The same boys will follow us closely as we walk up stairs and try to pinch our bottoms.

Mrs Kuzminska, the needlework teacher, is slim and old

and Polish with lots of blue-tinted silver hair and orange lipstick. She wears fitted suits and matching accessories. She is the oldest teacher in the school. I think she is also the most stylish. She examines my handiwork. 'You are good,' she says. 'You have an eye for detail, for design, you are patient.' She looks at me over the top of her glasses. 'You have found your vocation.'

I smile at Selina, who sits on a desk sorting buttons because she is no longer allowed to use the sewing machines. She takes no notice of the compliments I am given. She keeps on sorting the buttons into piles. Mrs Kuzminska asks her to stand and do a twirl and tells her, 'Yes, dear child, you have been blessed with the looks of an angel – and such ankles . . . you could be a model.' Selina gloats for days. 'You, dressmaker,' she sneers, 'me, mod-el,' and she raises her chin into the air and runs her hands down the sides of her body.

selina's new walk

She has learnt to walk so that her heel drags slightly on the floor before she takes a step. She has had metal half-moon shapes put on her heels so she clicks and taps as she walks. Everyone knows where Selina is. She leaves a trail behind her. Scuffing the school corridors. Scraping the polish off the assembly-hall floor. Making sparks on the pavement.

Selina woz here.

I wanted to have metal tips put on my heels. Selina said it would bring attention to my pigeon toes. I didn't even know I had pigeon toes.

The song the older boys sing to Selina as she walks across the playground:

> *Baby, let's get together*
> *Honey hush, me and you*
> *And do the things*
> *Ah, do the things*
> *That we like to do, oh . . .*

> *Do a little dance, make a little love*
> *Get down tonight, get down tonight*
> *Do a little dance, make a little love*
> *Get down tonight, get down tonight . . .*

The song the younger boys sing to Selina as she walks across the playground:

> No, you'll never get to heaven,
> No, you'll never get to heaven,
> In a Playtex bra,
> In a Playtex bra,
> Coz a Playtex bra,
> Coz a Playtex bra,
> Won't stretch that far,
> Won't stretch that far.

the story of the coat and the earrings

The coats we have to wear for school must be black. This is
the only specification. I decide that I am going to make
myself a black coat but in velvet. I make a sketch of the coat
I want. It is going to be beautiful. The shoulders are high
and slightly puckered, remembered from the pictures I have
seen in the library of a 1940s style. It is double-breasted,
panelled and tailored like an army coat with a deep vent in
the back to mid-thigh. The collar is wide, almost to the
shoulder, making a deep V to the point of the lapels, which
run long to just below the breast. I have designed it like this
because I like to wear my shirts showing outside the coat. I
think this looks both smart and sexy. The pockets are open,
angled on the side, and the coat itself falls all the way to the
ankle. It is so long that I will have to lift it as I walk up and
down stairs. I like this image; there is something so princess
about it whenever I see it in films. My coat when worn open,
my hands in the pockets, will move with a graceful swing
and the wind will catch it and billow it out behind me like a
sail. Closed, with its four huge silver buttons, it will hug the
curve of my waist and fit snug on the hip. I see myself
swaggering down snow-filled streets, making heads turn.
Selina is beside me. Sometimes in the same coat, other times
in the standard school-issue duffel coat.

I hand her the drawing. She examines it from far and
close up, turns it round in her hands, squints at it. I know
she is not impressed with the quality of the drawing. Selina

is better at art than me. She is known as being 'ever such a good drawer'. Finally she hands me back the drawing. 'Yes, please,' she says, 'that would be divine,' all posh and refined. Because that is the way we will have to talk when we wear such things.

Mrs Kuzminska helps me cut a pattern and we calculate the amount of material it needs. It will take six Saturdays of shampooing hair to get the money to buy it. I write down on a piece of paper how much money Selina should put aside and make her pin it above her bed.

All summer, with every head of hair I wash, I think of my coat and imagine Selina and me swanning around the streets.

The sound of the velvet as I cut it is deep and lush. Selina didn't buy the material for her coat. She spent the money on a pair of earrings. They are big thick gold hoops. While I cut the sleeves out I can hear her say 'Twenty-four carat' as she shows them off to the other girls in the classroom.

When she showed me I said, 'But what about the coat?'

'What about it?' she said, and tilted her head up and swung her head from side to side so her gold hoops caught the sun.

The coat is finished. People stare at me when I wear it, as I knew they would. All sorts of people. Young, old, girls, boys, everyone. One day, a fancy-looking woman comes up to me in the middle of the street as we walk to school and she asks me which shop I got it from. I feel myself blush. 'I made it,' I say. 'You made it,' the woman repeats. 'That's amazing.' She starts to ask questions, how long did it take, how much did it cost. Selina stands beside me, she takes her hands out of her duffel-coat pockets and pulls her hair back so her earrings show. She swings her head from side to side.

The earrings glint but the woman doesn't notice. She is about to ask me to make her one, I know she is. She is about to say: 'How much would you charge?' 'We're going be late,' Selina says and drags me away. I glance back at the women, shrug my shoulders and smile at her in a sorry way. She shrugs her shoulders back at me, readjusts her handbag on her shoulder and walks on in the opposite direction.

It snows for the first time that winter, thick and heavy on the ground. I put on my coat and the hat I have made to match. I walk to school on my own. Selina has taken to spending her time with Jayne and she walks with her to school now. They are walking just ahead of me. Both of them in their duffel coats and platform shoes. Selina now wears her hair like Jayne, pulled into bunches that stick out from the sides of their heads. Their shadows run long behind them into my feet. I walk faster, the length of Selina's shadow body. They sense it and walk faster, and again her head is at my feet. I call to them to wait but they ignore me. Then suddenly they stop. I catch up, but they continue to ignore me as I stand by them. 'See ya, then,' I say, and walk on.

I can see them in a car side mirror. I can see why they wanted me to walk ahead of them: they are bending down, scooping up handfuls of snow, moulding them between their palms. They call my name. Sweetly. Try to make me turn round. They ask me to wait. I ignore them, keep walking.

Jayne throws the first one. I know it's her because she makes the same sound she does when she passes the ball in netball. A little grunt through her nose. It hits hard between my shoulder blades. Makes a dull thud. Selina's hits the back of my head, knocks my hat forward so it covers my

41

eyes. I pretend nothing has happened. I neither speed up nor slow down. I straighten my hat. I am a queen: I am strong in all times of adversity. I walk tall, shoulders back, head high.

All the way to school they throw snowballs against my back. Non-stop. Fast. Furious. I count them. They throw a total of thirty-one.

Just outside the school gates I look back. Catch Selina's eye. Smile. Jayne takes her chance. Catches me full in the face. Selina waits till I turn away before she throws the snowball she has ready and aimed.

When I am in gym, they come and steal it. The coat. The wire hanger all bent down from the force of the swipe. On the floor, nearby, one silver button. I put it in my mouth as I dress. Suck it, as if this will bring it back to me.

I know it is Jayne and Selina. Everyone in the changing room is whispering their names. I dress quickly. No one looks at me as I leave, go out into the blizzard snow just in shirtsleeves and cardigan. I walk across the playground to the tall black gate. Climb on to the low wall next to it; pull myself up, swing one leg over and then the other. Jump. I head to where I know they will be.

They are sitting right at the back of the café, drinking tea and burning holes into a paper napkin stretched over a glass. A penny lies in the centre of the napkin. Whoever makes the penny drop, loses. They burn holes one after another, taking drags in between.

'What do you want?' Selina asks, not looking up.

Arms folded and rigid with the cold, I say: 'I want my coat!'

'What coat?' Selina says.

They shake their heads and look into their cups of tea. They say they know nothing. But I can see the edge of

Selina's lip quivering, like it always does when she lies. I want to hit her, but I don't.

In the playground, what I thought were fresh footsteps in the snow are pieces of black velvet. I pick the pieces up as I follow where they go.

In the girls' toilets, the group of smokers part to let me through. I follow the trail of water and velvet into one of the cubicles. The girls grow silent as I go in. My coat has been slaughtered, torn to shreds, half of it down the toilet bowl, half of it on the floor. Some stuck to the wall, as if it put up a fight.

Jayne and Selina are still sitting at the back of the café. Jayne is melting a polystyrene cup with a match. Selina is reading a magazine. I hold up a piece of the wet torn velvet in front of them.

'Been fishin'?' asks Jayne. I slap her hard across the face. As she cries out, I force the rag into her mouth.

Selina laughs. She gets up and she puts her arms around me and draws me close so her hoop earring digs into my cheek. She whispers she forgives me and kisses me where the earring has left its imprint. It is a perfect circle. I am hers. She whispers that she is my best friend. Now. Always. For ever.

mirror ball

We're at the disco. We're dancing. Except Selina doesn't dance. She undulates. If she were to be laid on the ground she would be a snake and slither away. Her bare arms move gracefully about her, Indian goddess-style, fingers elegantly poised. Her hips sway. Her feet take short steps forward, back and to the side, toe to heel, bending full at the knee. She sways at the hip, follows with her shoulders, tilts her head, tumbles her shiny curls. She brings an arm up over her head and down as she tilts her head to the other side to commence the new cycle of undulation. She dances like this to every piece of music, speeding or slowing the pace to keep the rhythm.

The next record fades up. It's Gloria Gaynor. 'Never Can Say Goodbye'. Selina adds a little more drama to her arm movements.

I have tried to get her to dance the way the other girls do. The way I do. With more bump and grind, with shorter, more frequent foot changes, with less arm movement. But Selina prefers her way. 'More sexy,' she says. She thinks that the way the others girls dance is clumsy, ungainly, unfeminine. I am included in this comparison. She imitates me, slouches and stamps her feet. 'This is you,' she says, 'and this is me.' And she starts to sway her hips again. If she danced the way I did we could dance the same dance together, as the other girls who are best friends do. I have tried to dance like her but I feel silly rather than sexy. My hips seem to jerk about rather than run smooth. I know that she prefers it if I don't dance like her because this is her dance. She has worked hard to perfect it. She doesn't want to share it. It makes her stand out on the dance floor.

Last Saturday night she danced with Bill. She kissed him during the slow dance and wrote down her phone number on his hand in eye pencil. He rang her every night at eight like he said he would, but she made me pick up the phone and tell him she wasn't in. Every night I had to say, 'She said to try again tomorrow.' I talked to him but watched her as she sat on the bottom stair playing with her split ends. I said, 'Sorry,' before I put down the phone.

'Why do you say sorry?' Selina said. 'I didn't ask you to say sorry – I'm not sorry – treat them mean – keep them keen.' But every day on the way to school she asked me if he had sounded at all upset or angry.

'He sounds the same every night,' I said.

After a while she'd ask again. 'Not all angry then, not at all upset?'

Tonight she dances with JB. She dances very close to him, putting her knee between his; sometimes she dances against him so all her parts touch his. She dances with him in the same way she danced with Bill last week. But as she dances with JB she stares at Bill, who sits in the far wall booth drinking lager straight out of the bottle. Earlier, when we arrived, she ignored him, looking the other way when he came over to say hello. She let him buy her a vodka and black but wouldn't dance with him. She said she was tired.

Bill sits in his dark corner. The glitter thrown out by the mirror ball above the dance floor cuts his face and body into little squares. Only bits of his face can be seen at a time. His mouth is small and angry. His eyes are wild. They stare back at Selina. In between his drinking he takes drags on his cigarette. For a moment his face is completely lit up.

JB knows that Selina keeps looking at Bill. He dances her around so her back will be towards him. Selina knows what JB is doing and plays along, dances with her back to Bill, dances as sexy as she can. She dances long enough to allow JB to catch Bill's stare. Bill raises his bottle in mock salute and drains it in one gulp. He tilts his head right back and his face turns purple under a light that had been previously lost in his dark black hair. He leans forward and slams the empty bottle down. He sinks further into his corner and lights another cigarette. He has five empty bottles lined up in a row on the table in front of him.

Selina dances herself around again so Bill can see her face. She smiles at Bill in the dark and then she smiles at JB. Bill moves forward into the light. She makes a coy gesture, pushes her hair behind her ears with her sparkling varnished nails.

'Hurt So Good' is the next record the DJ puts on. Selina has asked for this to be played for her. A quick dedication goes out, 'For Selina', and then the volume is pushed up high. I can't remember who sings it. Selina likes reggae. It's the thing she dances best to, she says. She mouths the words as she dances.

Bill gets up to get another drink. He pushes through the dancing crowd. On the way back from the bar he brushes against Selina. She pretends not to notice. She moves closer to JB, nuzzles her face in his neck. I can see Bill's fist clench tight around the neck of the bottle and the muscles in his jaw round as he grits his teeth. He disappears back into his dark corner, lights another cigarette. He doesn't look happy or sad. He looks like he's gone into a coma.

I am dancing with George. He will dance with any girl just as long as he is dancing. There are no ulterior motives. There will be no kiss at the end of the night. We dance alongside Selina and JB.

The record changes. David Bowie's 'Golden Years'. His voice is deep and low.

> *Don't let me hear you say*
> *Life's taking you nowhere angel* ('angel' is sung high like a girl)
> *Come get up my baby*
> *Look at that sky – life's begun*
> *Nights are warm and the days are young*
> *Come get up my baby –*
> *There's my baby – lost that's all*
> *Once I'm begging you*
> *Save her little soul*
> *Golden years, gold whop whop whop*
> *Come get up my baby.*

There is a specific dance that goes with this song. You move from side-on to your partner to face to face with a sort of bobbing hip motion. Inside hip when side-on, outside hip when face to face. The emphasis is on the height of the bob, the force of the bounce, all twists are done on the ball of the foot.

George and I stand side-on, shoulder width apart. We hold hands. We set our feet slightly wider than hip width. We wait for the beat and begin. We, along with half the dance floor, will maintain these movements for the entire track.

My body knows this dance without watching my steps. I watch Selina instead. She dances her dance for the first few lines, adding a bit more twist to her foot movements, and then she decides she is going to sit this one out. She gives me a friendly bump with her hip and smiles as she passes by.

She leads JB to the booth that Bill sits in. She slides along the seat beside him, squashes close. JB sits next to her, puts his arm around her shoulder. Bill offers her a cigarette. JB lights it. She smokes and nods her head to the music and sips at her vodka and black. Bill rearranges the seven empty bottles that now line the table. He fiddles with the foil at the top of the bottle, pulling chunks off and discarding them. JB watches the dance floor and keeps beat with his hand on the top of the table. The lights are being turned lower. The next record will be the slow dance.

JB and BM. That's how they introduced themselves to us last week. We pretended we didn't know who they were. There is not a telephone box or subway in north London free from their initials in foot-high red or green graffiti. None of the school sheds are without their mark. They are a living legend. They are even mentioned in the local papers. One is not named without the other. They are best mates. They are a team. JB is tall and thin. Bill is shorter but stocky. He is slightly bow-legged but better-looking than JB.

Selina had fancied Bill. She kept putting her hand under her chin when she was talking to him and she pronounced every word very carefully like she does when she wants to impress. JB and I had sat together while they danced and he had talked and I had listened, but I thought he was boring. He had listed the locations of the various cigarette vending machines they'd broken into and bragged about how much they had made reselling them. He gave me a free packet of Consulate but I was glad he didn't ask me to dance. They told us they were at the same school as us. We both knew that. Again we pretended we didn't know. We said we'd never seen them there. Which was sort of true. They were hardly ever there and, when they were, they hung around the 'big boys'' shed to play cards and smoke. No girls went there unless invited. They are older. Fifth-formers, they said. They'd seen us around, they said. They looked at Selina as they said this. All the boys fancy Selina.

Earlier tonight I had been dancing with JB. I didn't want to dance with Jayne. And last week Selina said as we walked home that I should dance with JB if he asked me. 'It would be like twins marrying another set of twins,' she said. He asked me to dance when Bill asked Selina if she wanted a drink. I smiled at her as I followed JB out on to the dance floor. She didn't smile back. After one dance she signalled for me to go to the toilets with her. She dragged me into a cubicle with her and locked the door.

'You're not to dance with him,' she said. 'It's about Bill,' she said.

'What about Bill?'

'I have to test him,' she said.

'Test him, what do you mean, test him?'

'I have to dance with JB.'

'You have to dance with JB! But last week you said I was to dance with JB if he asked me and he asked me.'

'If he – if Bill – if he really loves me . . .' she said.

She hadn't told me that he loved her.

'Has he told you he loves you?'

'No! Shut up and listen, just listen.'

She had her hands around each of my wrists. She yanked at my arms each time she spoke. She pulled harder as if this would make me really understand.

'If he really loves me, he'll . . .'

'He'll what?'

'He'll show me, he'll let me know.' She hissed the words close into my face and then backed away, let go of my wrists and leant against the wall. I scanned the various 'we woz here' signs that made up her background, saw our names in black Magic Marker just above the toilet roll and wondered what she thought Bill was going to do, this boy she'd only met the week before.

'So do you want me to dance with Bill, then?' I said, not sure of exactly what it was she wanted me to do.

'No,' she said. 'You're to dance with George.' She unlocked the door. 'It's sorted, he's waiting just outside.'

As she put on more lipstick and checked herself in the mirror I told her JB had been nice to me. He said how pretty I looked in my boob tube. Said I was clever because I'd made it myself. He bought me a Bacardi and Coke. He gave me two packets of Embassy, because last week I had told him that was what I smoked, not Consulate. I still thought he was boring but I didn't tell her this. It just felt good to be paid some attention.

'He's waiting for me,' I said.

Selina sighed heavily, swore and repeated that I was to dance with George. 'It's very important to me,' she said, looking at me with very sincere eyes. 'Very important,' she repeated. 'I hope you understand.' She instructed me to wait for a few minutes before following her out.

George grabbed my arm as I came through the door and pulled me on to the dance floor. He knew all the words to the song and sang along as he danced.

> *Will you take me – by the hand*
> *Tell me I'm your lovin' man*
> *Will you give me – all your love?*

51

And do it babe – do the best you can
Oh that's the way aha aha I like it aha aha,
That's the way aha aha I like it aha aha . . .'

I guided George and our dance so we ended up next to Selina and JB. JB looked sheepishly at me when he saw me. Selina won back his attention with a thigh-to-thigh rub. His eyes glazed. He was transfixed.

They danced continuously one record after the other. They danced to 'Jive Talkin' and 'Right Back Where We Started From' and 'Fattie Bum-Bum' and 'The Hustle' and 'You Sexy Thing' and 'The Bump' and 'Do the Busstop'. All the time that Selina danced with JB she looked at Bill. When 'Get Down Tonight' came on, Bill had got up and walked towards them. This was the record that he first danced to with Selina last week. Selina saw him coming and pulled JB's arms around her. She wouldn't look at Bill at all, turned her head away, only to stare at him again as soon as he took his place back in the dark booth. JB had just smiled at Bill, lifted one hand off Selina's waist, showed his palm.

The three of them now sit there in the booth. None of them seems to be talking to each other. They are waiting for the slow record. Bill drains another bottle of lager. JB lights a cigarette. Selina swirls the ice in her glass. Slow records are when couples kiss.

'Golden Years' is coming to its end. The lights are being turned down low. The mirror ball turns slower. Rod Stewart's 'I Am Sailing' fades up. Girls' arms wrap around boys' necks, boys' arms around girls' waists, one of the boys' hands always falls slightly lower to skim the curve of the girls' buttocks. Each couple starts to shuffle round in small circles. Some of them snog. Eyes closed tight. I see JB slide out of the booth, followed by Selina, followed by Bill. They stand there, all three of them, the mirror-ball reflections gliding across their bodies. JB and Bill are glaring at each other. Selina is waiting. She looks at the floor. Bill starts to slip his arm around her waist. JB lays a hand on her shoulder. George suddenly pulls me closer and blocks my vision to the booth. I can't see who Selina has moved towards. Who she has chosen.

I hear glass smash. Short and sharp and then delicate as someone kicks shards across the floor. Everyone has heard it. The dancing stops. The kissing stops. Someone on the dance floor screams. I see JB as he falls to his knees. His hands cover his face, blood seeps through his fingers, falls in big globules on to his shirt and on to the floor. I run to Selina. She is on the floor among the shards of glass. Her arm is cut. A piece of glass sticks out of the wound. She picks at it unbelieving and watches Bill. She cowers as he leans over her to put the broken bottle back on the table. He lines it up with the others, checks to make sure it is straight and then turns to Selina. He looks like he is going to hit her. I put my arms protectively around her head. He bends down close and whispers, 'Slag.' He walks past her to JB who is being tended by another girl. She has coaxed him to take his hands away but he keeps repeating that he can't see. She has cleaned his face with water and tissue. Only the bridge of his nose is cut, but it is deep and it continues to bleed, running into his eyes, blinding him.

'C'mon,' Bill says to him, and pulls him up without looking at him. He snatches the tissue from the girl's hand and gives it to JB and then guides him across the dance floor to the exit. The crowd parts to let them through. Rod Stewart is still singing 'I Am Sailing'. Selina looks up at me. There is a small smile on her face.

53

JB's scar

JB's scar is shaped like an apple pip. The fat bit by his left eyebrow, the tip at his right. It is deep and bright pink. Selina says it is better than him having a tattoo of her name on his arm. He will never forget about her. He will see her every time he looks in the mirror and Bill will remember her each time he looks at JB. She is indelible. Like Magic Markers.

notes

My mother has grey-blue eyes.
I have grey-blue eyes.

A chromosome is a coiled structure in the nucleus of the cell.
A chromosome is a single DNA molecule.
A single DNA molecule consists of two single strands
    wound around each other.
It is a double-helical structure.
Each strand is made up of four nucleotides.
A linear section of DNA molecule is a gene.
The gene is the basic unit of inheritance.
Each chromosome carries a large number of genes.
In humans there are twenty-three pairs of chromosomes in
    each cell.

Meiosis is the cell division which results in the daughter
    cells having half the number of chromosomes present in
    the original parent cell.

Meiosis produces the sex cells: the gametes, the ovum and
    the sperm.

She is an Aries.
I am a Gemini.
She is fire.
And I am air.
My favourite lesson is needlework. Followed very closely
    by biology.

I am going to make wedding dresses.

I am going to make virgins for Gabriel (this part is secret).

Selina's favourite lesson is art. Followed very closely by biology.

In art she draws two things: still lifes or many-headed monsters.

She had to have six stitches in her arm.

She kept them when they were taken out.

In the glass box with the brass frame.

The one that I gave her.

When the scab formed she picked it off.

Three times she did this.

I thought of mitosis as it healed.

Selina always gets mitosis mixed up with meiosis.

Mitosis is the cell division that produces identical daughter cells.

Mitosis is Selina and Me, her mother and my mother, all sitting at Selina's mother's kitchen table shelling peas.

Selina's mother has brown eyes.

Selina has brown eyes.

sex education with mr jenson

He talks about his three kids as he starts to demonstrate how to put the condom on the perspex see-through penis that stands on his desk. The sunshine is casting a rainbow penis shadow large on the wall and his shadow hands upon it make it look mythical. Like it were the ghost appendage of some long-ago giant.

'They were all planned, all three of them,' Mr Jenson says of his children as he unrolls the gossamer pink deftly with thumb and finger to the base of the model. He stands back a little from the desk and looks at the result. 'This should always be done,' he says in clipped tones, 'prior to copulation,' and he writes 'prior to copulation' down on the blackboard in capital letters and underlines the word 'prior'. The chalk hitting the board sounds like his voice. Then he casts his blue eyes across the boys who sit at the back of the classroom.

He has wavy blond hair and a pale angular face, a full mouth and long fingers that he usually waves about his head as he talks. But his eyes are far too far apart so sometimes he reminds me of a fish. Other times he looks pretty enough to be a girl. When I tell Selina this she looks at him and then at me as if I am mad.

The boys at the back of the classroom stretch and twang their condoms like rubber bands and speculate about their use as catapults. 'Prior, meaning before, for those of you not sure,' Mr Jenson says in a loud voice. The boys look up for a second and groan. We girls who always sit at the front of the class fondle the flimsy bits of rubber skin and make warm or disapproving noises.

'Just like real skin,' says one girl touching it.

'Disgusting,' says another.

I sniff at the greasy pink latex and run it between my fingers. It smells like pear drops.

Selina pokes me in the ribs so I have to look at her. She is holding hers taut over her mouth so it flattens her lips. She makes cross-eyes and forces her tongue out against the pearly pink. Mr Jenson coughs in the way that only teachers can. Selina removes the condom from her mouth, rubs her mouth on the back of her hand.

'Tastes interesting, sir.'

'The idea is not to eat it, Selina,' he says.

'Not what I heard, sir,' she says.

The whole class collapses into laughter across the dark brown science benches, which leave bits of old flaky yellow varnish on their cheeks when they lift to take a breath. All laugh except Selina who has put the condom into her mouth and starts to chew it like gum. She gets up and prances up and down the aisles between the benches, tilting her head side to side as she chews.

Mr Jenson watches her. He leans back on his desk, folds his arms and sucks in his cheeks as if he is trying not to smile. He watches her for a full three minutes. And I watch him. I decide that what I find so attractive about him, even if he does sometimes look like one of the fish which swim in the tanks against the back wall, is that he knows what is going on in my body. It gives him a sort of power as if he has X-ray vision. I wonder if the other girls think like this too. Probably not, although they do look at him through glazed eyes a lot.

60

The boys at the back blow up their condoms or split them with their fingers and force them over their faces. They come to the front of class where we girls sit and push their new alien faces into ours and make us scream and we kick them in the shins or bite their arms. I am trying to concentrate on Mr Jenson. He is watching the clock. He waits until the second hand hits twelve. His voice booms over the riot. 'ENOUGH.'

The class quietens. Last to quieten is Selina who makes sure to make as much noise as possible with her stool as she gets back on it. She spits the condom out. Holds it up against the light. It is full of teeth marks and holes.

'Not much good now, sir,' she says.

There is a small round of giggling at the back, but the girls know better. Our discarded fun lies in a small pink shiny pile in the middle of the bench. Mr Jenson points to the bin by his desk. Again she scrapes her stool as she gets up. She walks up to the front of the class very slowly carrying the condom by its tip, never for a moment taking her eyes from Mr Jenson's. She is doing the walk that we do when we practise how to be catwalk models. One foot directly in front of the other to create a hip swagger. She gets to the desk and drops the mauled item into the bin. It makes a soft squelch.

Mr Jenson folds his arms.

'Pick up the bin and go and collect everyone else's.'

Selina does as she is told. But she holds the bin on her head and resumes the swaggering walk as she circles the room. I watch Mr Jenson watching her. Again sucking in his cheeks. Holding back a smile. I am as good as Selina at this specialised walking. I get up to join her, play follow-the-leader, one hand on my hip, the other holding an imaginary bin. I manage to take five steps.

'Very good, Maddy. Now sit down.'

Selina is asked to do the next demonstration of putting on a condom. She can't do it. She is all fingers and thumbs. One of her long nails rips a long slit in the side. But she doesn't want to give up. She gets a fresh one and fails again. And I am so pleased. I watch and pray that she won't get it right. And she doesn't with the third or the fourth attempt. The class mocks her: 'C'mon, Selly.' We start to sing: '*C'mon, C'mon, C'mon, C'mon . . .*' She shouts at us to shut up and makes those eyes at me that mean 'I'll deal with you later!' I shouldn't have sung along. I go quiet.

I look at the female companion to the penis. Also perspex, it sits at the other end of the desk, its shadow lost in the bones of Nelly the skeleton that hangs from a hook in the corner by the blackboard. For the male, the hard perspex seems right. For the female, wrong. It should be made of velvet. I look at Nelly's child-bearing hips. At least the suggestion of female space is there even in death. Can't say that for a man. As if she knows I am talking about her, Nelly rattles in the breeze from the open window and her hand, the one with two fingers missing, drags against the wall and against her sharp black shadow.

The class is still taunting Selina and I can hear Mr Jenson is all the time telling Selina to ignore us, to stay calm, to focus. Then he helps her, using his hand to guide hers over the penis model. I see this in the shadow on the wall. His hand on hers. I turn. I cannot help myself.

'Should you always get the man to help, sir?' My voice sounds angry, loud.

Mr Jenson doesn't bat an eyelid or remove his hand. And no one in the class laughs. Instead, they go quiet and I feel all their eyes on me. I look to Selina for help. Selina pretends

I don't exist like she always does when she is embarrassed by me. Everyone is waiting for Mr Jenson to speak.

'If necessary, Maddy, yes,' he says. He sounds exasperated.

And then together he and Selina resume and finish their task.

'Well done!' he says.

There is a small round of applause and one of the boys at the back makes a comment about volunteering the real thing. I tell him to shut up.

Mr Jenson asks Selina to stay after the class has gone. He wants to discuss her earlier disruptive behaviour. There is a small window in the door to the biology room and I can see her slumped across a bench kicking restlessly at the bottom of it. She fiddles with one of the gas taps, turning it on and off. I wish she'd breathe a little deeper each time she turns it on. Mr Jenson asks her to stop. So she gets up and sits on his desk and plays with the model penis instead, drifting her fingers up and down and round its girth. I hear him say, 'What is wrong, Selina?'

I have heard him ask this question a million times. It is the question he asks all of us if we misbehave, or haven't done our homework, or look sad or look tired. He tells us we can talk to him about anything. Anything at all. He says it as he chews the tip of his pencil. Periods, boyfriend problems, girlfriend problems, parent problems or, on a lighter note, he even offers fashion tips. Because he knows that 'you girls worry about these things'. He suggested once that Selina would look best in black. But to lose the heels as they could damage her spine. Selina only wears black now but hasn't lost the heels. 'Only bores wear flats,' she says. To me he says blue. Because I am so pure. This is what I tell Selina.

'Well, you bloody would be, wouldn't you,' she had said. In fact, he never suggested any colour to me. He told me I looked wholesome enough to eat. 'A fit young lady like you,' he said, 'never need worry what she wears.'

I wait for Selina to respond to his question. She gets up again and smooths down the back of her pencil skirt. She ignores him. Turns her back on him, readjusts her hair in the reflection of the window, wets her finger and runs it along her eyebrows. She is saying something but she is talking quietly, almost whispering, so I can't hear what she is saying. She gets her bag and moves towards the door and makes a face at me.

'Nothing is wrong, Pete,' she says, turning back to him for a moment.

She is only supposed to use his first name at home when he comes with his family for Sunday lunch. Then he says, 'Good afternoon, ladies,' to me and Selina. I think that if he wore a hat he would remove it and bow. And then we say, 'Good afternoon, Pete.' His wife is her mother's best friend. 'Just like you two,' Selina's mother likes to say to describe their friendship. His wife is the one that wrote the anatomy book. That's how they met. She went to him for advice.

Selina is out the door before Mr Jenson can say anything. Selina knocks on the window in the door and waves good-bye. Mr Jenson has a strange expression on his face. He looks suddenly sad. Defeated.

I ask her what she said to him. But she says, 'Oh, nothing.' Very casual and relaxed.

precautions

The family-planning clinic is on the second floor of an old Victorian building. It is next door to the clinic for sexually transmitted diseases. A woman wearing a white coat and thick glasses shows Selina and me into a small room. On a desk she has the same models that Mr Jenson has in the biology room. On the wall are various internal diagrams of a man's and a woman's sexual organs. The woman sits us down. She takes all our details. She tells us it's all confidential. She puts her hands on her lap and smiles at us. She tells us that if we are going to indulge in sexual practice and want to avoid pregnancy we have the following choices: they are laid out on the table in front of her. She picks them up one by one.

The Diaphragm: It looks like a rubber version of a flying saucer.

The Copper Seven Coil: Made of copper and shaped like the number seven, this could lead to heavy and long periods.

The Oral Contraceptive Pill: She stresses that they have to be taken every day. I like the way the blister for each tablet has the day of the week stamped on the metal foil at the back.

Condoms: We know about these.

It is suggested that in any event to avoid pregnancy we always use condoms. We are each given a plastic bag full of them to take with us.

I am fitted for a diaphragm. Selina says that she'd like to go on the Pill. She thinks that it's very grown up to take a pill every morning. She knows it will impress the other girls when they see the packet in her make-up bag. I also know she has no intention of taking them. She has no intention of doing it yet. We are both still virgins. Mr Jenson suggested that we come here and get sorted out – just in case. He put his hands lovingly on our shoulders as he said it. 'Be prepared,' he said.

gabriel

The whole room is filled with the heavy sweet scent of the lily. He leaves the lily behind in the room when we walk but its perfume stays with him. Tiny bits of orange pollen dust his hands and his wings. He always smells of lily.

Under his pink robe he wears a long saffron dress. As he walks it kicks out in front of him and falls back inside and under the pink robe. He walks steadily and surely as if each time his feet touch the ground little roots grow out of the bottom of them and take hold beneath him. His toes are long and pale. There seems to be no weight in his step at all. He walks with his hands behind his back, his right hand resting in the palm of the left. With each of his steps the thick silk of his robe makes a swishing noise and the gold-braid edging glitters.

Under his saffron dress there is another garment. White. A triangular strip of it shows from the elbows to the wrists on the back of his arms.

I like to watch him walk. It calms me.

The colour of his hair changes with the light. Sometimes it's blond. Sometimes it's red or strawberry blond or golden. It falls in soft ringlets against his shoulders and in between his wings.

There is always the slightest blush in his cheeks.

Attached to his robe below his wings, and at the front at his waist, are lengths of gauze. They float about him as they catch the breeze. Sometimes the one in the front floats up high enough to veil his face.

We follow the curve of the river bank. I walk without shoes. The grass is thick and cool.

We haven't said anything to each other.

We have just been standing on the ramparts of the castle in the wind for hours.

Listening to the wind.

Gabriel's robes beating about him like a flag.

My hair stormy around my head.

Watching.

The tips of the trees in the forest swaying.

The clouds scudding low and fast.

The river going from silver to dark as the wind turns the water over and back.

His hand on my shoulder.

For hours and hours and hours.

Until it gets dark and the moon comes out.

I sense a presence, something darker in the black.

Near the bridge Its eyes catch the light.

I see only Its eyes. I sense Its vast body.

I hear It move towards the river's edge and slide into the water.

Its wake lapping at the shore.

A dull watery echo under the arches of the bridge as It sinks into the depths.

The moon climbs higher in the sky; the river becomes still. Glows silver.

Gabriel runs his hand down my arm and takes my hand.

We walk back. I watch our shadow on the water.

I can visualise every internal moment of sex. It makes for useful revision. Even after the exams, I do it for years like a chant in my head. Testes, Seminiferous tubules, Primordial germ cells, Spermatozoa, Sertoli cells, Vasa efferentia, Epididymis, Vas deferens, Urethra. Some of them I never could pronounce properly. When they orgasm I spell out in my head – E-J-A-C-U-L-A-T-I-O-N. And there it is inside me, a swarm of wet, sticky, white tadpoles.

boyfriends

I like quiet boys. The ones who say little but know a lot. Know the names of things. The sort of boys that sit on their own in libraries at lunchtime.

The quieter they are the more my interest is aroused. In particular, there is John.

I bring sweets bought by the quarter from the corner shop. These quiet boys always like sweets. Liquorice Allsorts. Lemon Sherbets. Pear Drops. Flying Saucers. Black Jacks. I put them all in one paper bag for possible finger-touching. But he waits until I take my sweet before he takes his. 'Thanks,' he says very softly. I lick the sugar from my fingers. I smile as I do it. Tilt my head to one side as he looks back at his book.

The sweets click-click against our teeth; today we both chose lemon sherbets. I drag my chair a little closer.

'So what you reading, then?'

He shows me the cover.

Quiet boys read: Astronomy, Aeronautics, Aerodynamics. They all seem to want to be astronauts.

'Can you tell me what a galaxy is, then?' I curl a strand of my hair around a finger.

He finds a picture in his book to show me. A mass of white haze against black that looks like it is swirling. I take the sweet from my mouth and read out the words, my sticky finger following them, leaving small smudges of dirt. I have to lean into him to do this.

'A galaxy is a system of many thousands of millions of stars, together with interstellar gas and dust.'

I put the sweet back in my mouth.

'I can never imagine a million things – can you?'

He pushes the sweet into his cheek.

'That's because we've only got five fingers on each hand – people can usually only imagine or remember up to five things in their memory; after that they just say many or lots – or have to count on the rest of their fingers.'

'Oh?'

He holds up his hand to prove his point. I put my hand on his, palm to palm. He freezes, gulps, waits. He is thinking of something to say. Anything. He says: 'Stars that are moving away from us are red-shifted and stars that are approaching us are blue-shifted.'

I slide my hand so my fingers are in the gaps of his. He relaxes a little. He crunches his sweet as our hands drift back to the book. He turns the page to show me another picture. We are back out there. Far away in the stars and the moon. Everything is fine again.

On the way back to class it is quiet, there is no one around. I slip my arm around John's waist. I kiss him in the grey hollow-sounding corridor and in the afternoon-light stairway full of window-frame shadows and later against the damp dark wall in the alleyway walking home from school. It is no use waiting for quiet boys to make the first move. It is not in their nature. He doesn't know whether to keep his mouth open or closed when he kisses me. When his tongue reaches mine, something inside him cracks. I can almost hear it happen. He makes tentative moves with his hands, outlines my body with short pats to the breast, the thigh, the bottom. His hot long fingers tremble at the hem of my skirt.

'It's OK,' I say.

Selina doesn't like it when I go courting with my bag of sweets. She waits for me on the bench in the playground, her arms folded, or hangs around the sheds, smoking cigarettes. If she can't find anyone to keep her company, she will come and stand outside the library and bang hard on the wired glass, squash her mouth on it, stick out her tongue. She'll keep doing this until I go and join her. Selina used to try and get off with my boys. But she doesn't do that any more. Not since she started going out with Steve Baker, her brother's best friend. He's tall, black, handsome. He's at a different school. He comes to meet her at the gates at home time. She brushes her hair, changes into her high heels and they go off together, her arm through his, to the café for fags and sweet tea.

John and I don't go to the café. We sit on the wall outside his house.

'What you thinking, then?'

'Clouds, just looking at the clouds.'

'Oh – do you know their names?'

He takes his hand out of his pocket, stretches his arm and points a finger to the heavens.

'Those are called cumuli.'

The clouds are fluffy, drifting slowly against a blue sky.

the first time

We did it at John's place while his parents were out, in his single bed. It had a green candlewick cover.

I remember the sound the condom packet made as he tore it open with his teeth. The purposeful movement his head made. The muscle in his neck. The small regular movement of his right shoulder blade as he put it on.

I was not nervous. Or excited. It was as if I was not really there.

Afterwards, the smell in the room was like the smell of electricity gone wrong.

John got up.

'I have to go for a walk,' he said.

We dressed and went downstairs. He showed me into the kitchen.

'Make some tea, I'll be back in a minute.'

He was gone for an hour. He came back with a bag of lemon sherbets and a smile.

phases of meiosis (illustrated)

A Interphase

Cell in normal non-dividing condition with chromosome long and threadlike

B Early prophase I

Chromosomes contract, becoming clearly visible. Nucleolus shrinks.

C Mid prophase I

Homologous chromosomes come together (synapsis) forming a bivalent

D Late prophase I

Each chromosome seen to consist of a pair of chromatids

E Metaphase I

Chromosomes arrange them-
selves on equator of spindle

F Anaphase I

Homologous chromosomes
part company and migrate to
opposite poles of the cell

G Telophase I

The chromosomes have
reached their destination and
the cell constricts across the
middle as in mitosis

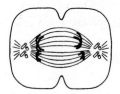

H Prophase II

The two daughter cells prepare
for the second meiotic division:
centrioles have replicated and
a new spindle is formed

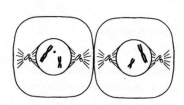

I Metaphase II

Chromosomes arrange
themselves on the spindle in
the usual way

J Anaphase II

Chromatids part company and
migrate to opposite poles of
the cell

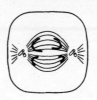

K Telophase II

Cell constricts across the middle
and the nuclear membranes and
nucleoli are reformed as in
mitosis. Chromosomes regain
their threadlike form and cells
go into the resting state
(interphase)

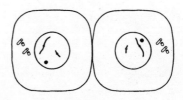

L Waitophase

Cell hopes for union with
like-minded cell of opposite
sex to regain sense of
completeness and corporeal
body

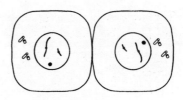

(Waitophase is Mr Jenson's joke)

Note: In the formation of the egg, the second meiotic
division occurs immediately after fertilisation.

sex determination (illustrated)

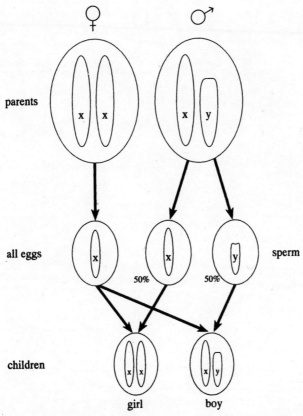

An individual's sex is determined by his or her chromosome constitution. A female possesses two x chromosomes in her cells. A male, one x chromosome and one y chromosome.

the he and the she and the it

I dream I am undressing Gabriel. Instead of his clothes, he is wearing bandages, like an Egyptian mummy. I unwind them, circling him again and again, very carefully, being sure to wind the bandage back into a neat roll with my hands. The first time I get to the skin, I am unwrapping bottom to top. There are his well-turned ankles, his legs long and smooth, his penis with crease marks along its length. Next, a flat belly, the outlines of his ribs and then springing up lightly as I ease away the bandage – breasts. I wrap him up quickly again in my mind and start again. This time it is the other way round. A vagina and no breasts. I try again. This time there is everything of both sexes at the same time. I touch the breasts and then the penis. As I touch them they retreat into the body like snails into their shells. The labia melt into one another, fuse and close. The body is left smooth. All his skin becomes like the white-pink skin under a freshly picked scab. Like the underside of a goldfish.

I have discovered that angels are sexless. I am heartbroken. Gabriel is the person I am loving when I have sex. He is beyond all the body, all the sweat and fluids. Gabriel is where I go to in my head. He is the one I summon inside me. He is the one who takes me to castles and clouds. He is my pin-up. And he is no longer male.

He is not female either.
I console myself.

1. In this non-sex state Gabriel is even more pure.
2. Gabriel can be whatever sex I want.

I feel the ping of ovulation each month. I imagine it sounds in my body like the timer on my mother's oven. I know which are the safe days and don't have sex on the days that aren't. I know all the facts. But I still fantasise that a tongue in the ear is what brings babies about. I've made it my own personal superstition. I am strict, not even a nibble on the ear lobe is allowed. I never worry about getting pregnant.

Selina is still a virgin. She says she is waiting for Mr Right. 'Sex' is the first thing I have done before Selina. I made sure of that. This makes me proud even if she does call me 'a slagette'.

falling

Behind the big plane tree at the end of her parents' garden, Selina sticks her tongue in my ear. Her tongue is small and slimy. She darts it in and out quickly like she is trying to catch insects.

'Do it properly,' I say.

'No,' she says. 'It tastes funny.'

'Let me do it to you, then.'

I turn her side-on. She holds back her hair with both her hands. As I slide the tip of my tongue into her, she falls to the ground laughing hysterically.

Saturday 17 July 1976

Selina is a cliché; she has gone from virgin to mother in one fuck.

I always knew she would. I put my hands on my hips when she tells me and say to her face: 'You're a cliché.'

I kneel down beside her on the grass. The smell of sick on her breath is overpowering, made more pungent still by the intense heat of the day. In front of her, the pink plastic baby-doll bath stands half-full with yellow and orange vomit. The irony is not lost on her. She catches my eye, raises her eyebrows and gives me a knowing smile. I smile back. But I'm not happy.

Selina is fifteen. Selina is pregnant. I want to lie her down and peel away her stomach, to see what is growing inside her, just like our pop-up anatomy book. I want to know if its hands are in prayer. She is twelve weeks gone, as they say. The swell is just beginning to show. Without thinking I lift the front of her T-shirt. Her hand clamps around my wrist. She looks at me perplexed. Tightens her grip.

'What do you think you're doing?' she says.

She uses both her hands to move mine away, deposits it on my lap.

'Sorry,' I say. 'I just wanted to see it.'

We tug at the grass, rearrange our legs, shift our weight. The roar of a plane fills the sky. We both look up, wait for the plane to come into sight. Watch it until it disappears for what seems like for ever.

'OK, then,' she says, and she lifts her T-shirt and shows me her belly. She takes my hand and places it on the roundness, uses her hand to smooth mine across its surface and round in a small spiral.

'So you're gonna keep it?' I ask.

'Yeah,' she says. Her mouth all smiles. Her voice all expectation.

'And your mum, what does she say?'

'She says – if I'm happy, she's happy.'

'Are you happy?'

'Yeah.' She smiles and sighs all at the same time.

She is going to be sick again. A wrench undulates her body, throws her head forward. I hold her hair back from her face. My hands full of her thick brown curls. I want to pull it, yank it hard, but don't. She gets her hair cut. I get my hair cut. I buy a dress. She buys the same in a different colour. I can't go to the shop to get a matching baby.

'Whose is it?' I ask.

She tuts but doesn't say anything.

I ask another question. 'Why didn't you tell me before?'

'Just because . . .' she says.

'Because?' I stare at her. She stares back. Blinks once. Widens her big brown eyes.

'It's none of your business!' She turns her head away from me.

This hurts me. We have always shared our secrets. Again we rearrange our legs, shift our weight. I finger my hair, bite my lip.

'Can I touch it again?'

Slowly she turns back to me. Offers me her body.

91

'Go on, then.'

I put my hand back on her stomach. It lifts up and down with each of her breaths. My hand X-rays her insides, brings me a picture, a line drawing of a foetus, biology homework. Sexual reproduction. It has legs and arms, hands and feet, fingers and toes, a face with lips, a large forehead, eyes, a stub nose. The forehead can wrinkle, the head can turn. It has kidneys that produce urine. It is probably four and three-quarter inches long and weighs about four ounces. There are breathing and swallowing reflexes. It is inside Selina. Already her trousers are too tight. A thick ridge of flesh falls over her waistband. Selina and I used to have exactly the same waist size, the same bust size. I look at her breasts. I don't know why I haven't noticed before. They are bigger, fuller. I poke one of them with my free hand.

She lifts a shoulder to her ear.

'So you won't be able to borrow my clothes any more?' I pat her belly, pinch the extra flesh.

'Yeah – suppose so.'

'S'pose this means you'll be leaving school?'

She raises her eyes to the very blue sky and lets out an impatient sigh.

'Silly girl.'

'That's rich,' I say, 'coming from you.'

She pushes my hand away from her stomach, lies down on the grass, her bare belly to the sun, and closes her eyes.

'Shut up, Maddy.' Her mouth goes very tight.

She opens her eyes and stares at me for a long time and I feel something inside me slowly diminish like the white dot on the television when I turn it off late at night. I sit there in my internal darkness waiting for something else to take its place. The diagram of the penis I have to do for part of my homework fades in.

'Where did you do it?'

She lifts her hand and extends her arm. Her finger points in the direction of the big tree at the end of the garden.

'Behind there.' She says it matter-of-factly, but proudly.

'Who with?'

'Who with, who with?' She imitates me.

'Don't tell me, then – I don't care.' I get up to leave. 'I really don't care.'

But I care very much. I want to know who has taken my friend away from me.

'Don't go,' she says. She takes my hand again. She pulls me down to her side.

'Steve Baker.'

'Steve Baker – but you said you were never going to do it with him.'

She shrugs her shoulders and sighs. 'I know – but, well – you know . . .' Her smile is naughty.

I put my hand back on her warm stomach.

'What do you want – girl or boy?'

Selina slips her hands beneath her bulge, lowers her head, talks towards her stomach. 'Don't care,' she says.

She looks up at me. Suddenly a thousand miles separate us.

Sunday 18 July 1976

I get up out of bed and the idea of me follows. I try to walk and I fall down. If I move my head I want to be sick.

The doctor shines a special torch in my ear. I have an

infection, a virus, in the labyrinth of my inner ear. The virus is paralysing all the tiny hairs that grow there. They can't detect the movement of a fluid that moves each time I do. They can't send the signals to the brain about where my body is in the world: if I am standing up, if I am lying down, if I am falling.

I have to stay in bed until the virus goes.

I have to keep very still.

Selina watches me from the doorway. She won't come in. She is scared she may catch the virus off me and start to fall down even though the doctor says it isn't contagious. She pats her belly, says she has to think of the baby.

I wish pregnancy was contagious.

Gabriel and I stand on the ramparts of the castle. We look down into the valley and fields. We watch the boats move up and down the river. In the distance I can see the yellow eyes of the beast.

I want a baby. I would like it so me and Selina have a baby at the same time. I imagine them playing together in the garden and me and Selina pushing our prams around the streets and feeding them together and sharing their clothes. I would like a baby too.

Gabriel takes me by the shoulders. He looks me straight in the eye. He speaks slowly and clearly. 'You are only fifteen, Maddy, you have your whole life ahead of you. Enjoy your youth and freedom. There is plenty of time.'

Selina gets bigger and bigger. I walk to school on my own. She wears her mother's clothes but won't give me her old clothes to wear. She spends her time looking through catalogues and paints charts, teaches herself how to knit. Her bedroom is full of piles of little clothes. Steve Baker is still at the school gates at home time, but he goes to the café with Jayne now to smoke fags and drink sweet tea. Jayne tells me that Steve says he never touched Selina. She says Selina is a liar, so I slap her face.

'Just you wait,' she says, and scurries off.

Selina's brother doesn't talk to Selina or Steve any more. I meet him sometimes in the corridors between lessons. He always used to say hello; now he just nods his head at me. I walk home with my sister instead of making her trail behind me. Selina is pregnant and I suddenly have a sister.

In the dead of the night Selina throws stones against my window. I meet her in the garden to find she is crying. She leans against me as we walk, her head on my shoulder, sobbing. I ask her what's wrong. She says nothing, sniffs loudly, drags her nose across the bottom of her T-shirt, exposing her eight-month swell.

We sit behind the big tree. It is very dark. All I can see is her outline. She takes both my hands in hers and I can feel her stare at me.

'Tell me,' I say.

'Secret,' she says.

'So tell me.'

She shakes her head. Takes her hands back, folds her arms, then curls up and puts her head in my lap. She asks me to stroke her hair.

'Can't tell you – not ever.'

The next day at school Mr Jenson has a black eye.

Her mother has bought the crib, the buggy, a week's worth of nappies. The nursery has been painted a bright yellow. The baby is born and the baby is given away. No one sees it. Not even Selina. I'm not allowed to visit her in hospital. My mother won't tell me why. She just says Selina's mother said Selina changed her mind. Selina's brother phones me up. He says Selina has asked him to tell me not to ask any questions.

The nursery is painted white again. The crib and buggy are taken back to the shop. Selina's mother comes to the school. Her shouting can be heard all the way in the playground and that afternoon we are told that Mr Jenson will no longer be teaching us science. Selina comes back to school. She tells everyone the baby died and cries at playtime in the loos as she smokes her cigarettes. Some of the other girls flick cigarettes at her ankles and call her a slag. 'You made him do it to you,' they say, 'you was always touching him.' She gets one of them by the hair, puts her head down the toilet and flushes it. 'Anyone else?' she says, lighting another cigarette. She is not called a slag again. Steve Baker and Jayne break up. He waits for Selina at the school gates. Ten Number 6 and a chain with a love heart as a peace offering. I watch him lift her hair and put it round her neck.

Selina and I don't talk about what happened to the baby, even when she shows me the silvery stretch marks it's left on her stomach, her buttocks, the sides of her breasts. She only knows that it was a boy, that he weighed seven pounds and eight ounces.

the purification

Selina and I get in the bath. We wash our hair and put the conditioner on and wrap towels around our heads. While it seeps we apply our face packs. We wait for them to harden. No talking. I use cucumber and Selina oatmeal. Her skin is dry; mine greasy, as she always reminds me. We rinse our hair and wash off our face packs. We shave our legs and underarms. We towel-dry our bodies. We blow-dry our hair. We pluck our eyebrows. Thin. Arched. We rub in our body lotion (pale pink Johnson's). We put on our skin-tight T-shirts, identical, matching except for the colours. We do our make-up. We do our eyes the same. A heavy black outline of kohl. Two layers of mascara. Then we put on our jeans (Wrangler's) but don't do them up yet. We need the pliers for that. Selina is first. She lies on the floor. She holds the zip together as close as she can and I straddle her and grab the zipper with the pliers and tell her to take a deep breath in. I help her up. And then it is my turn.

We have to do squats to loosen up the jeans so that we can walk properly. Selina counts them out loud. We do ten; our hands firmly placed on our thighs. Then Selina practises her undulations in front of the mirror. We are ready.

It is Friday night. We are going to the disco.

influential friends

spanish dave

Selina has met a man. He is called Spanish Dave. He has a moustache that forms three sides of a square around his mouth and sideburns shaped into a thick wedge. Spanish Dave blow-dries his black layered hair so it stands up from his head and wears a black three-quarter-length coat whatever the weather. There is always a cigarette hanging from his lips and he sniffs constantly. Spanish Dave is a drug dealer. Acid, Sulphate, Moroccan, Thai, he can get it all, he says. Since meeting him Selina has learnt to make the perfect joint in double quick time. She even carries a tiny pair of scissors to cut the roach and trim the end. She says that she's not interested in the other stuff.

Spanish Dave takes me and Selina to Soho with him. We wait in the car and smoke cigarettes. It's so cold all the windows have misted up. Selina draws a heart in the mist with her finger. Empties its middle. Writes her name above and Dave's beneath it.

'How can you possibly fancy him,' I say, 'he's such a creep.' I tell her how I couldn't ever imagine doing it with anyone like him.

'He's very nice once you get to know him, very gentle,' she says, writing his name again.

'And,' she says, 'he tells me he loves me all the time. All the time,' she says again looking at me. A stupid coy smile on her face.

I'm about to say something else about how old he is, he

must be at least thirty, but she tells me to shut up because he's coming back. She can see his face in the vacant heart that is steaming up fast. He smiles as he opens the car door and talks through his cigarette. He does not have a deep voice with a foreign accent to go with his Latin looks. His voice is soft and full of Liverpool and everything he says sounds like a question. He always puts his right index finger to his temple when he speaks, as if he is thinking very hard. He used to wear a gold signet ring on this finger but Selina now wears it on her wedding finger. It was too big for her so she had to bind the back of it with cotton. When I asked him once why he was called Spanish Dave he had to put a finger on each temple. After what seemed a very long time he said: 'My best mate, he's called Dave, and my mum, she's Spanish – all right.' He says 'all right' a lot and frowns as he says it. I don't know whether Spanish Dave has a bad memory or is just really stupid. Selina says it's because he's always stoned.

Spanish Dave leans into the car. He says he's going to be longer than he thought. Do we want to come with him and wait inside where it is warmer? 'Told you he was thought-ful,' Selina says as we walk the sleet-covered pavements. My feet are getting cold and wet. I think of my chair in the English lesson just by the radiator. Mrs Mison would be reading chapter six of *A Passage to India*. I get angry with myself for agreeing to spend the day with Selina and lag behind contemplating how I can make an escape. But Selina keeps looking round and smiling, making happy little shrugging movements. I watch how proudly Spanish Dave guides her through the crowd, his hand huge on her back, and the way that she leans her head against his arm.

I follow them through the streets. Big pictures of half-naked women surround every doorway. They have their fingers in their mouths or are cupping their breasts or touching in between their legs. Big hair. Big breasts. All their bodies looks alike, only the hair colour seems to vary. All their facial expressions look the same as if they are sharing the same pained moment. There is a lot of lip-licking. Selina and I, we have been to Soho before, to get dress material from Berwick Street or walking through as a short cut from Oxford Circus to Leicester Square. We are not shocked. The pictures are no different from pictures on the newsagent's top shelf. Sometimes we imitate the more silly poses. We are approaching a picture of a girl on all fours; the picture is taken from behind. She is cocking her leg like a dog about to pee. Her head stretched peeking around her shoulder, her tongue out, her eyes rolled to the sky. She is touching herself. I stop. I call out to Selina. I cock my leg. I point out the picture. She looks at it. She raises her eyes to the sky like the picture but she tells me to keep up because 'Spanish Dave is late'.

We walk past open doorways on which are pinned cards with the word 'model' scrawled in childlike fancy writing or printed in neat capitals. Next to 'model' is an arrow that points up or down. Selina turns and gives me a quick look: there is a prostitute standing in a doorway. She has blonde hair. She is wearing a see-through shirt with no bra, fishnet stockings, a tight short skirt, high heels with ankle straps. She looks just like the way we've seem them on telly. Her make-up is heavy. She is smoking and she tilts her chin up as she inhales. She catches the eye of every man that passes her and smiles. She looks away when I look at her, throws down her cigarette and stubs it out with her toe. She turns and goes inside and a man follows her. They disappear into the dark of the corridor.

Another street. Shops whose entrances have curtains made of coloured strips of plastic. I catch glimpses through the gaps. I see the back of men's heads as they read magazines and pictures of naked women lined up in neat rows on the racks against the walls. A whole row of a woman in a dog collar eating an ice cream.

Spanish Dave and Selina stop at a doorway marked out in bright flicking lights. Before we go in, Spanish Dave says, 'You can go home, Maddy, if you want.' He points his finger down Brewer Street. 'The tube is just there.' His expression is sympathetic, but Selina suddenly looks frightened. I see her give a little shake of the head. 'No, it's OK,' I say. And we go in.

In the doorway a girl wearing hardly any clothes sits behind a tiny reception, reading. 'Next show's not for an hour,' she says, not looking up. Spanish Dave says, 'It's me,' and runs a finger along her arm. 'Hi, lover,' she says. Her smile is huge. Selina looks at me anxiously. 'She probably says that to everyone,' I whisper to her. 'He's back now,' the girl says to Dave and points her thumb behind her.

Spanish Dave tells us to go on down. But we wait for him to take the lead. The staircase is narrow and steep, goes on and on, deep under the street. It gets darker, the light bulbs turn red and the stench of stale cigarettes sticks in our throats. We have to concentrate on our steps. Our high heels make no noise on the sticky carpet. We run our hands against the greasy walls to keep our balance and Selina snags a nail on a torn piece of wallpaper.

'Fuck,' she says.

Spanish Dave tells her it doesn't become her to swear.

She tells him to 'Fuck off', and 'I'll swear as much as I fucking cunting want to'.

He stops and turns on the stair. He looks defiant. We stop as well. They stare at each other for a while.

'Do you want me to go?' Selina says finally.

He smooths the side of her cheek with a hairy hand. 'You know I don't, my love.'

'Well, shut up telling me what to do, then.'

He leans towards her and kisses her where he has just touched her and as he does she nudges me with her elbow.

I poke her back to affirm her triumph. And we continue.

We are in a small empty cinema. Thirty or so seats. Everything is red. The walls, the seats, the carpet. The smell is rank. I can smell semen. Fresh and old and dry. There are white stains across the old velvet. It stinks. 'I'd rather stand,' I say when I'm told I can sit down. I can't even bring myself to lean against a wall. From two small speakers on either side of the screen badly tuned radio music is being piped in. Dave disappears through a doorway below one of the speakers. 'You wait here,' he says as he closes the door. Selina gets up on the platform and starts to do her sexy dance. She tries to entice me up there with her with spidery come-hither fingers. I smoke one cigarette after another, pace up and down the narrow aisle; think of going out of another door which has an exit sign above it.

'Let's go,' I urge Selina.

She is wiggling her bum.

'No way,' she says. 'I need a bit of something, know what I mean.'

I know she has some hash in her purse.

'But you've got some,' I say. Think about asking her to roll a joint to calm me down.

'Nah – not talking about that, talking about a bit of . . .' She snarls up her nose and sniffs loudly.

She had promised me she wouldn't. By the tone of her voice I know she is already familiar with what she wants. She has lied to me. I make for the staircase we came in by to leave. At exactly the same time Spanish Dave reappears through the door.

'C'mon, girls,' he says.

'I'm going, Selina,' I say.

Spanish Dave puts his arm around my shoulder. My body does not crawl at his touch as I would expect; it tingles. The tingle goes all the way down my spine. I let myself be drawn closer. Try to keep back my smile. I see Selina watching and make myself duck out of his hold and stand some distance away. Stare at the exit sign. His bulk blocks my escape. He looks at me.

'We're all going,' he says, 'but first . . .'

From his coat pocket he pulls a tiny paper envelope, waves it at Selina, who rushes to him, eyes agog. She gets out a mirror and a blade from her bag, opens the packet with deft fingers and uses the tip of the blade to shovel a small white pile of powder into the centre of the mirror. I have never seen her concentrate so hard. She chops at the pile and with the same rhythm that my mother chops parsley. Then she separates it out into three lines. She fusses over them like they are a work of art. Each must be identical. So she pats at the ends, moves a bit here, moves a bit to another line. Dave has been busy rolling a pound note.

'Get a move on,' he says.

Selina goes first. She makes Dave hold the mirror and scoops back her hair, firms it behind her ears. She holds one nostril closed, inserts the rolled pound note up the other. She looks to me. 'Pay attention,' she says all nasal-like. She

108

hoovers the line in one strict sweep, taps the residue from the note, wets her finger and collects it, brushes it on the front of her teeth. It makes her make an ugly face. The sort she used to scare me with when we played monsters.

Dave goes next. The first time I see him take his cigarette out of his mouth. And then it's my turn. I deliberate. I'm curious. I unfurl the pound note and smell it. It stinks like rancid cheese.

'Smells like your feet, Selina,' I say.

But Selina can't manage a smile. Her mouth has set into this sort of rictus. Straight across as if she cut it there with her own blade.

'Go on,' she says. Her voice is all calm and detached.

My logic tells me the sooner I do it the sooner we get out of this place.

It feels like someone has put fire up my nose and poured something acrid into my mouth. It tastes vile and immediately my mouth loses its pliability and my teeth become self-conscious. They need to grind.

'It's disgusting,' I say, hardly moving my lips.

And then the rush hits me. Suddenly I am incredibly warm and I want to go and I want to stay all at the same time. I don't know what I want to do but I want to do something. Selina looks over at me. Her face is ironed of all expression. I know mine looks exactly the same.

'Shall we go, then?' she says stiffly.

'Yes, let's go,' I say equally stiffly.

Back out on the street everything is now bright and cheery. Everything is super-interesting. All the naked women are sharing the same pleasure. My cold feet no longer bother me. I like the way I can feel my heart beating fast against my chest. I want to talk to Selina about how we are going to do our hair, what shoes we'd like to buy, but she and Dave keep stopping for what seem like eternities to snog.

In the car I'm not sure where we are going but I don't care. The radio is loud and as long as we are moving and there are things to see out of the window I am happy. The journey can't go fast enough and I don't want it to end. I am irritable, restless and content. Selina says she knows what may help and hands me some chewing gum. Spearmint.

We go to Spanish Dave's place. He lives in a block of flats in Belsize Park. The block is identified with a huge number. Number 49. Each digit is at least three feet tall. I want to make a joke about it, but I know there is no point because my body feels like it is beyond laughing. Like every cell in my body is rigid, as if they are standing to attention waiting for the next instruction.

He lives at the very top. The penthouse, he calls it. I can see St Paul's and the Post Office Tower from the kitchen window. The kitchen is where they make me wait while they go and do it.

While I wait, I clean. Clean everything. The cooker, the stove, the fridge, the floor, the windows. The insides of cupboards as well as the outside. I unscrew the handles with a knife to get to the hidden bits of grease and dirt. I Brillo-pad the screws.

I can hear them having sex behind the closed door of the bedroom. They seem as if they are never going to stop. I can hear Selina telling Spanish Dave to hurry up. They both make groaning sounds. Then it is quiet. I hear her say my name. I tiptoe over and listen. Selina is asking him why he put his arm around me. She is telling him she should be the only one.

Spanish Dave went to Prison. That was what Selina said to the girls from school when they asked where he was. She enjoyed the way they put their hands over their mouths as she told them. She looked sad as she told them the news. 'I write to him every week,' she added. 'No', she has not made any promises to wait.

They nodded their heads in understanding: she had already left school for him. Just before exams. It would be too much to expect her to wait.

It is all lies.

It is all lies, except the bit about school. Except how sad she is.

One day Spanish Dave went to Soho and did not come back.

He phoned her from a call box in Liverpool. In between the pips and the 10p's.

'You have to be out of the flat by the end of the month,' he said.

'You don't love me any more?' she asked.

'You're too much hard work,' he told her.

She took me to a church to tell me. Lit a candle. Something Spanish Dave did sometimes for his dead dad and when he felt religious, she said.

'This is for Dave,' she said.

She lit another. She did not say who it was for.

'I need a smoke,' she said.

We sat in the graveyard, on a tombstone, underneath a yew tree. It was cold enough to see our breath. From her bag she got blue Rizlas, Silk Cut cigarettes, Swan Vesta matches, her tiny scissors, and arranged them all neatly between us. She unzipped her ankle boot, produced from the point of its toe a small plastic wrap of grass.

'Roach,' she said to me. Very quietly.

I used my cigarette packet: she does not like to damage her own. I passed her a cardboard spiral. She unfurled it. Rerolled it.

She was not as quick as she usually is. She took her time. I wanted to tell her to hurry up, the cold was moving closer to the bone. The sound of her fingers against the paper was rough and dry. They moved round and round. She rolled it and rolled it before she licked. She smoothed it across its length with her fingertips. She wanted it to be perfect. It was perfect. It looked factory-made. She snipped the end. We watched the tail fall into a crack. She wedged the plastic wrap in after it. Forced it with a match. She had used all the grass. It was enough for three.

She lit up and leant back and inhaled the smoke in three short breaths. Held it in.

'Bastard,' she said as she exhaled.

She brought her index finger and thumb to her mouth to touch a tooth: they have started to wobble; too much speed.

We were three-quarters of the way through the joint before she spoke again.

'He got me a flat in Camden Town.'

She waited until I inhaled. Waited until I was holding it in.

'Two-bedroom,' she said.

'Two-bedroom,' I said as I blew out the smoke. I nodded my head and smiled at her.

112

It was the closest she'd get to asking me to move in.

She put her hand out to take the joint, took a couple of puffs and handed it back.

'I always said he was considerate.' She stated it like a fact as she stared up in the dark canopy above us.

'What are you doing?'

She had brought her hands to her neck, she was taking off the chain she was wearing, the one Steve Baker had given her with the heart.

'First time I've done this,' she said as she gave it to me to hold. She took the last couple of puffs of the joint and stubbed it out.

She pulled off the ring Spanish Dave had given her, the one she wore on her wedding finger. It came off easily even though she had had it made smaller to fit. She threaded the chain through it.

'Help me put it back on,' she said.

She held up her hair and turned away from me and I fastened it round her neck. You couldn't see the heart any more, it was eclipsed.

She put her boot back on and stood up.

'Let's go,' she said.

The next day Selina had the ring engraved on the back. It says: *Dave 1978–1980*. On either side, a love heart.

our new clothes, our new looks

Blondie's 'Parallel Lines' fills the flat. Selina plays it all the time. She puts it on first thing in the morning, turns it up so loud the windows vibrate and I worry the neighbours will complain. She sings along while we get dressed.

Our new clothes. Our new looks.

Suede ankle boots with a thin heel like Chrissy Hynde, like Siouxsie. Narrow-leg jeans, second-hand 1960s Marks and Sparks cardigans with tiny white buttons worn back to front, PVC coats – in black or white, or both. Even when it doesn't rain. For warm summer days, a choice of shifts in psychedelic colours, jelly shoes with glitter, bright plastic necklaces made from beads in the shape of fruit. (Selina wears hers over her chain, over the ring and the heart). For autumn days, tweed skirts, thick ribbed tights, black stilettos, something mohair on top, an oversized coat. Our hair is short, spiky, the tips bleached and pinked with crazy colour. Our earrings are big and long. Sometimes we wear just one. Bangles grow up our arms. We dress up to go to the corner shop to get a pint of milk.

Selina has been to the dentist.

Her teeth no longer wobble.

Selina has to smile a lot: Selina is a waitress. She has been a waitress since she left school.

She spends her days saying:

'How would you like it done? – Rare, Medium Rare, Medium, Medium Well, Well Done?'

'Pommes Frites or Jacket Potato?'

'Salad? – Mixed? Green? Tomato and Onion?'

'Which dressing would you like? – Blue Cheese, Thousand Island, French, Mayonnaise?'

'Water? – Sparkling or Still? With or Without ice?'

In the background plays Ella Fitzgerald or Frank Sinatra or Nina Simone. The tablecloths are gingham; there are framed prints of black-and-white photographs by Atget and Brassaï on the wall. The floorboards are bare and varnished warm brown.

Selina works three days a week and four evenings. Alternate Saturday nights.

'Smiling is very important,' she tells me.

She takes pride in her work. She is a good waitress. Makes the best cappuccino. Gets the best tips.

Before I go to college, I go with her to her work. If it is warm, we walk. If not, we take the bus. It is not far, just off Camden High Street. Almost a straight line. We buy breakfast on the way. Usually a croissant, sometimes a diversion to get a tahini bun from the Greek bakery. We also buy cigarettes. Selina smokes Silk Cut. I smoke Marlboro. Selina makes me her extra special cappuccino with its mountain of froth and extra chocolate, and I sit and read the paper and eat my breakfast or watch her and the other waitresses set up.

There are three waitresses on during the day. One of them takes down the chairs; Selina always sweeps the floor, another one mops. As they wait for the floor to dry they fill the salts and peppers, polish the cutlery, separate with expert speed the paper tablecloths, laying their arm along the perforations and pulling and putting them to one side, they fold napkins with fine precision, bringing the corners to meet exactly, sliding the hand across. They make small Leaning Tower of Pisas as they stack them one on top of the other. Then they lay the tables. Selina has told me sometimes they do it in a round, one following the other. One putting on the tablecloths, the other the napkins, the other the cutlery; the one who put on the cloths then puts on the glasses, polishing them, holding them up to the light to check for smudges. The one who did the napkins then places the salts and peppers, the small vases of flowers – usually a carnation or another type of flower which has a long life – and then the ashtrays. Other times like today, they take a section of the restaurant each and lay it out. Selina is meticulous. She straightens each knife, each fork, makes sure the glass is exactly right, makes sure the settings are exactly opposite each other, symmetrical. She makes sure the spacing between the salt and the pepper and the ashtray and the vase are just so. Every one of her tables is identical. You would think her life depended on it.

She steps back when she has finished to view. She smiles. It is gleaming, sparkling, fresh and clean. Waiting.

She straightens some of the glasses in the other girls' sections as she moves towards the coffee machine to stack the cups and saucers. The other waitresses, exchanging raised eyebrows and an amused smile, say nothing, as if it is expected.

She refills the coffee beans, one girl checks the sugars, the other sets up the station with its separate piles of cutlery. Selina banters with the boys in the kitchen as she walks back through the restaurant to place a missing knife.

'You look tired, Selina. Hard night?'

'Yeah, some of us are luckier than others.' She talks as she walks, turns her head to say it, winks at the boy, who juts his head up, throws his tea towel over his shoulder as he laughs. The other waitresses who have overheard also laugh. Selina, it seems, is popular but she never brings anyone from work home. Never sees them outside work.

Because Selina is artistic, she gets to do the daily blackboard. She uses angular neat capital letters and coloured chalks to decorate it with flowers. She has learnt various food words in French. *Champignon* is her favourite. She says it with precision. Holds it in the nose.

When she has finished, she joins me at the staff table where I have been drinking my coffee and folding napkins. She smokes a cigarette as she changes from her heels to Chinese slippers with the bar over the top. She has to wear black for work. She folds her apron shorter on the bar. Although the apron is long, the management expects her to wear it short.

'Like me fanny cover, Mads?' she asks as she puts it on and ties it. She shimmies towards me. The other waitresses laugh. From somewhere in the kitchen, an unseen male voice with a foreign accent.

'I'd cover your fanny any day, Selina.'

The manager, who is sitting within earshot, coughs. He looks at Selina out of the corner of his eye. Selina puts her hand on her hip and bends at the knee in mock threat, looks in the direction of the manager and then in the direction of the kitchen and the unseen kitchen boy, shakes her head. They all love Selina.

The staff table is cleared and laid up. I have to move to the bar. All three waitress, including Selina, disappear with their bags, return with make-up refreshed, lipstick re-applied, pen and order pad slipped behind the strings of their apron. They lean back against the bar on their elbows in preparation. Selina looks as perfect as the table she's laid. The door of the restaurant opens. A girl with a weak smile walks in. Selina immediately moves to meet her.

'Are you Selina?' she says.

Selina smiles. 'Are you the new girl?'

'Yes.'

'See you at home, Mads,' she calls out.

''Bye, Maddy,' the other girls call out.

I wave and go.

'Get some toilet roll.' It is Selina shouting at me, as the door is closing behind me.

Selina does not like my fashion school friends.

She does not want them round at the flat.

Ever.

'They're up their own arses,' she says, whenever I mention any of them.

She has only met them once.

princesses

A toile is an exact copy of a wedding dress. It is what is made first. What the changes and alterations are made to before the real dress is made up. Usually it is made in calico. It is fitted to the bride-to-be and then it is taken apart, the pieces used to cut the fabric for the dress.

When the dress is made up, an underlining and lining are put into place. The underlining offers invisible support. The lining makes it fall as it should.

Lady Di is helped out of the carriage.

The dress is too fancy. The skirt too big. There are too many frills. Lady Di doesn't look like she has a body at all.

I wave my spoon at the television as I say what I think.

Selina, Kate, my sister, and I are watching the wedding, eating Rice Krispies.

'I think she looks beautiful.' It is my sister speaking. It is only the second time she has spoken since our mother dropped her off at our flat. Kate is twelve; she has had her haircut done the same as Di's. She puts her spoon down in her bowl and runs her hand through her hair after she has said it.

'You think she's beautiful?' Selina says, her tone indifferent, her eyes fixed on the telly.

My sister eats the last spoonful of her Rice Krispies and drinks the remainder of the milk. 'Yes,' she says, not looking at Selina, her eyes straight ahead on the screen. On Di.

'Do you think you're beautiful?' Selina glances towards me in anticipation of Kate's answer.

'Walked into that one.' I smile at Kate, ruffle her hair.

'Well, are you or aren't you?' Selina watches Kate out of the corner of her eye.

My sister says nothing; she looks into her bowl she is holding close to her chest and then looks towards me.

'If you got her haircut, you must think you are.' Selina's voice rises, gets sarcastic as she pushes her face close to my sister's ear.

'Selina!' I stretch my arm out across my sister and push Selina away. Selina seems shocked. She leans back. She puts her bowl down. She folds her arms.

'Do you think Kate's beautiful?'

'She's my sister.'

'But is she beautiful?'

Kate is looking at me. Her face is anxious. It is saying, 'Please, say yes.'

Selina is looking at me. Her face is mocking. It is saying, 'She looks exactly like you when you were twelve.'

On the television Lady Di's train comes to a halt. The congregation settles. The ceremony is about to begin.

I sigh. I lean back out of their gaze. Kate gets up and turns up the volume and sits down again between Selina and me. Selina slides off the sofa to sit on the floor.

'So what do you think, Selina? – do you think Kate is beautiful?' Kate looks at me as if I am mad to bring the subject up again.

Selina does not look back as she speaks. 'Beautiful, no – pretty, yes . . .' she says. You can hear the smile in her voice.

Kate and I both smile huge smiles. The two of us grow warm with the glow the news brings. Kate slips her hand into mine and squeezes it. Underneath all the smiling, I feel a bit sick.

Selina slides her body back on to the sofa. She looks round briefly towards both of us and turns back to the television.

'Nothing make-up couldn't improve.'

We watch the rest of the ceremony in silence.

She holds the strip of foil with her left hand. The lighter with her right. The empty Biro container is already in her mouth. She has put Sellotape over the little hole. She brings the foil closer to her face, ignites the lighter and inhales.

It takes about ten minutes. Sometimes fifteen. She walks as she waits. She sits and she waits. And then she moves slowly through the flat. It is as if a mist has filled her body. As if the smoke expands in her insides and takes over all the space inside. She stills. Her breathing slows and quietens. Her skin tone seems to even. Not so much white as opaque. Like the frosting on a light bulb. Her eyes glaze over, the pupils narrow, the lids grow heavy, blink frequently as if she is about to fall asleep. All her limbs relax. There is space between her shoulders and ears that is not normally there. Her smile is lazy. She is happy. She is mellow. She has not a trouble in the world. I like Selina when she is like this. It is like Selina but smudged around the edges. Soft. Fuzzy. It is Selina but with the volume turned down.

scissors

Selina still keeps Spanish Dave's ring, threaded on to the chain that already holds the heart Steve Baker gave to her. She wears them 'in between', as she puts it. 'In between' is never very long. She slip-slides from one to the other. Overlaps for a month until she is sure that her new landing place is a safe bet. 'A foot in two camps,' she says. Selina is constantly with her legs apart.

She meets them everywhere. Tube trains are her speciality. Furtive glances that grow into conversations and exchanged telephone numbers. One out of every three she meets when we do our stall at the market at the weekends, my clothes, her cards (she could sell dust with her smile). Selina likes men that are tall. She likes it if when they put their arm around her it can rest easily on her shoulder.

She makes them all think that they are the 'one'. She says that she'll never ever leave them. She doesn't leave them alone for a second, she phones them twenty times a day. 'I am dead without you,' she says to them, taking their faces in her hands. From the moment they tell her they love her Selina is hunting for the next. Long tube journeys. Selina goes through her men like a hot knife through butter.

She never spends a night at their places. She always brings them back to our place. I hear her say the same things to each one of them through the thin walls that divide our rooms.

She says, 'You're the best thing that's ever happened to me.'

She says, 'You're very special.'

She sounds very sincere.

Her bedroom is pink and red and gold. Frills and chintz and brocade. She favours brass beds. The ones that stand high off the ground. High enough to hide under. Not that she ever does. She keeps everything very neat and tidy. Fresh sheets for each new fuck.

I tell her that sex too soon leads to a false sense of intimacy. She rolls her eyes at me and tells me to become a nun. Seeing as I always go for the monkish types. She cuts her foil as she says this. She uses my pinking scissors because she likes the neat zigzag. Later, the flat fills with a sweet yellow smoke. I tried it once. Didn't like my sudden oblivion to the world. She says one day she'll stop. No one knows except me. All her men have been clean since Spanish Dave. Solid types. Not quite tweed jacket but approaching it. Still a leather jacket here and there.

Once, I think she suggested a threesome. Nothing explicit, just a certain smile thrown at me and a beckoning nod of her head as she went into her bedroom with one of her men. She waited a while, just staring at me. I said nothing and she closed the door.

She has a strict routine. She sees her man on Mondays, Wednesdays and Fridays. On Tuesdays she meets me from the bridal shop, where I work part-time, and we go and see a film then on to a cocktail bar. She drinks black Russians. I like tequila sunrises. On Thursdays we prepare for our stall. I run up skirts and trousers and tea dresses. Selina makes cards. We do the stall on Saturdays and Sundays.

adele

It is Adele who makes Selina want to stop taking heroin.

I hate and love her for doing this.

I am twenty-three. Selina twenty-four. Adele is only twenty.

Adele looks like her name sounds. A bell. Or rather the suggestion of a bell. Her shiny blonde hair is cut into a bob, which curls out at her shoulders and sways from side to side when she walks so you expect her head to ring. The sound that she would make if she were a bell would be a delicate lingering tinkle. Adele, tall and willowy, has gentle green eyes beneath a high forehead. When she laughs she laughs only through her long narrow nose. A light humming that soars and drops to the back of her throat. Her rosebud mouth keeps firmly closed, her high forehead smooth and still.

Adele's mother is Italian. Her father is a Scot. She has her own pasta-making machine and a marble pestle and mortar and she grows basil in a pot on the window sill. When she makes risotto she likes to eat it straight out of the pan. When she sits in the sun she gets a strip of pale ginger freckles across her cheeks and the bridge of her nose.

Selina met Adele at the restaurant. Adele works in public relations and marketing. Her head is permanently inclined on a slight tilt from cradling the phone. It makes her look a little lost and pensive as if she is listening to some distant sound to place herself. It makes her look innocent.

127

Selina and I wear only black. We backcomb our hair to grand proportion, wrap our scarves twice to form a band. Between us we use a tin of hairspray a week. The clothes we wear have to be something baggy with something tight. Never both the same and never ironed. We make an effort to appear slightly mussed as befits the fashion. Ankles must always be exposed and the shoes flat, lace-up and chunky. Adele uses heated curlers and brushes her hair till it shines. She has a predilection for wearing brown trimmed with cream. She wears fitted suits with little gilt buttons and court shoes. Even at the weekends she wears these clothes. When she cooks she bothers to wear an apron. It is white and embroidered with red flowers. She removes her rings carefully one by one and puts them in a small glass bowl before she kneads the dough for the pasta. After washing up she uses hand cream for her long fingers and rubs almond oil into her perfectly manicured nails. Adele bathes twice a day.

Selina thinks that Adele is the height of Continental sophistication even if she does sometimes swear as much as adolescent boys on the top decks of buses. She even outdoes Selina. Everything is fucking this or fucking that. Her sweet honey voice makes 'fucking' sound as disgusting as it should – which it never does when Selina says it – and as if it were a product to sell. Her eyes widen when she says the word as if to give it illumination. Every time Adele swears it makes me want to tell her to wash her mouth out with soap and water. I notice how she never polishes her shoes and I do not like her pearl stud earrings. Selina covets her pearl stud earrings.

Adele is not one to judge. Adele is gentle and kind. Adele never talks about herself. She enquires after the health and well-being of others. And people open up to Adele 'like she is the sunshine and they are the flower', says Selina, which makes me sick. She never makes the problems her own. She doesn't offer her own equivalent experience. She doesn't try and solve it. She always seems to understand. Adele listens. Adele puts her hand on a shoulder and says, 'So what do you want to do about it, then?' Adele is a very good mirror. She is as shiny as her hair.

This is why Selina asked Adele to come and stay. Selina thinks that Adele can help her solve her problems. (By making her help herself.) She tells me she has never had anyone take so much interest in her life. I know, of course, I don't count. I am like family. I know too much. I can finish Selina's sentences.

Adele was leaving her 'man', as she called him, and needed somewhere to stay. It was only ever supposed to be temporary. She sleeps on the chaise longue in the living room. The one Selina and I found and carried home between us in the rain. The one I covered for Selina in red brocade with a gold-tasselled fringe, as she asked for. The one Selina spends her days lounging on when she isn't working. I told Adele this the first time she lay on it. Adele had given Selina a knowing smile. Selina looked to the floor. Feigned guilt. There was what I thought was an awkward silence as Adele readjusted her position, making sure to cross her legs at the knee and pulling her skirt over them. Then between them they had laughed so much they had to hold their bellies. Adele's humming laugh and Selina's low and dirty throaty roll. Selina had told her everything. About the drugs, about the many men. They were no longer just our secret. Selina's and mine. The laughing eventually faded out. They turned and gave me the sort of smile mothers give a sibling to reassure them that they are not being neglected or ignored.

Adele makes pasta with her pasta-making machine and pesto in her marble pestle and mortar. After supper she makes espresso for us in her little silver pot. She pours it into doll-size cups that are pale pastel blue and decorated with white polka dots. On each saucer she places a diminutive spoon and a miniature almond biscuit. The handles on the cups are so small that they can only be picked up with the very tip of the thumb and first finger and it seems to come naturally to sip at the coffee delicately from such a fragile thing. Adele smiles broadly as she watches Selina and me drink, our little fingers poised high in the air, as if she is pleased that her cups have produced in us a more feminine aspect.

Selina shows her how to do her make-up to make her eyes seem bigger and her lips fuller, but she must always use matt lipstick, nothing shiny, 'Understood?' Adele meekly nods. Selina suggests an alternative style for her hair, backcombs it and suffuses it with lacquer and gel, gets rid of the bell and replaces it with big hair. Adele smiles at her new self in the mirror, but when she comes out of the bathroom the bell bob is back.

I want not to like Adele and her goodness and kindness but I cannot help myself. Everything about her makes me smile. She charms me as she charms everyone else. Adele has no enemies. On her birthday I buy her a black polo neck and make her a long black skirt from a tube of jersey. Selina makes her a present of a diamanté brooch. I lend her some shoes and we go out, the three of us in black, to a club and dance. In the street she walks in the middle, a head taller than both of us. On the way home she whispers to me that she has a brother she would like me to meet.'

Selina is in awe of Adele. I can see it in her eyes, in all her body movements when Adele is near. Her body seems to get smaller. Even her voice when she speaks takes on a softer tone and sometimes she stumbles on her words. I have never seen her like this with any man. She never shouts at Adele like she does at me when she is in a bad mood. There are evenings when it is just Selina and me at home and she hardly talks at all. When I speak I hear my words too well. They sound awkward and searching and get little response. Then Adele comes home and Selina is up and about and making cups of tea and chatting nineteen to the dozen and I can't get a word in edgeways. And she sulks when Adele takes too much interest in me. I know that we get on better than Selina cares to acknowledge. And she knows Adele will not take sides. Not like Jayne used to. Adele, it seems, has become my friend too.

Selina waits for me to go to bed. Then she and Adele stay up until late in the night. Mostly it is the bass line of Selina's voice I can hear. Sometimes the perfect mid-tone of Adele. I can't hear what is being said. There are long intervals of silence and I know that Selina is crying. The next day Adele will ring me from work and tell me what Selina said and I will fill in the gaps.

I make it known to Adele that Selina will do anything to please her. She would stop taking the heroin if she asked her. It would be a sacrifice of love. She wouldn't ever do it for me. Yet I cannot talk to Selina for a week when she tells me that Adele has made her deal with the sense of hopelessness that made her want to take drugs in the first place. She announced proudly to me that she no longer felt the need. She hugged Adele in the kitchen and cried. I thought how the mighty have fallen. I watched Adele blush.

131

The doctor gives Selina pills to take. She attends a group once a week. It doesn't take long. It is not so hard. She never really was a full-time addict, I keep telling myself to make me feel better. But part of me had hoped she wouldn't succeed.

The bells are ringing . . .

Adele got Selina to enrol on a part-time graphics course; bought her a full set of Panotone pens.

Adele is all things beautiful.

Adele drew me up a business plan; got me a loan to set up a studio.

Adele says Maddy will make wedding dresses.

Adele says Selina will be an illustrator *extraordinaire*.

Adele is wonderful.

Adele is wonderful.

Adele whispers to me: stay single; she thinks her brother will be available soon.

If her arms are fleshy, suggest sleeves. If her hips are big, an A-line skirt.

If her shoulders are broad, veer her away from halter-necks and thin straps. If her legs are good, suggest a knee-length design. If she has a short torso suggest a Basque. If she is busty, advise a neckline that is open – scooped, square, V, or sweetheart. If she is of a larger size, show her fabrics that will drape her curves; guide her away from fabrics that cling or fabrics that are shiny.

Selina visits my new studio.

She walks around like she is the inspector of new studios. She lies on the new cutting table.

'Watch your shoes.'

'Don't be so precious.'

She flicks through the fabric books. She twirls the dummy. She snips the scissors open and closed, brings them close to her ear.

'They sound sharp.'

She leafs through the drawings.

'All very bridal.'

I am quiet.

She was going to model my designs but she changed her mind.

Her course three days a week. Her work three evenings. (Still the same restaurant: 'Better the devil you know than

133

you don't,' she likes to say.) 'No time.' She had waved her hand in front of her face.

There would be time if she wanted to.

We get the bus home. It is a fifteen-minute bus ride. Door to door. Selina points out the posters; states the typefaces they are in: Helvetica, Times New Roman, Palatino. She says things now like: three-colour process. CMYK. Tracking and kerning. Serif or sans serif.

If I am late at the studio, I pick Selina up on the way home. I wait at the bar as she clears her tables and puts up the chairs. She sits next to me, reapplies her lipstick and changes her shoes. She checks herself in the mirror and we go. We walk home. Sometimes we stop off at the garage to buy cigarettes and milk.

lorimer

Lorimer is Adele's brother. Adele introduces Lorimer to me one spring Sunday afternoon on Hampstead Heath. He looks incongruous in his quasi-gigolo get-up on top of Kite Hill. A suit, shirt open to his chest, biker boots. Six-foot two inches. He looks a bit like Elvis Presley, sideburns and a quiff.

I like the way he looks; I like the way he places his hand on the middle of my back as he guides me to the bench. He smiles more than he talks. A full smile. His voice is soft, mellow, hesitant.

He sits in the centre. Adele on one side. Me on the other. High above us the kites flutter and snap. I can feel the warmth of his thigh against mine. It runs straight to my stomach. When he looks at me I pull strands of hair behind my ears . . .

We are an item; our names are mentioned in the same breath.

Lorimer and Maddy.

Maddy and Lorimer.

Selina still wants to know why she wasn't invited that day.

She likes to tell Lorimer, each time she sees him, that he reminds her of someone she once knew and then she looks at me and gives me a closed smile and says, 'Don't you think?'

It is my twenty-sixth birthday. I am leaving the flat I share with Selina; I am going to live with Lorimer. Selina watches me from the doorway as I carry the boxes down the stairs; she doesn't say a word.

At a party Selina whispers dirty things to Lorimer. 'I want to fuck you,' she says, 'I want to feel you inside me,' her hands spider-creeping down his body to touch his cock.

He tells me later, what she said, what she did. Says he'll never do it. Has sex with me instead. I know she uses these lines on men. 'For a laugh,' she says. She read it in a magazine when she was twenty. Article title: 'How to Lay a Man'. She has been saying the lines ever since. I will say nothing to her because I know she will smile, lean forward, put her hand on my thigh and say, 'I was drunk.' I do what I always have done with her when I am angry with her. I make her very small and jump on her head. Till her brains ooze, her eyes pop out, her beautiful nose is shattered, her hair is covered in blood. While Lorimer and I have sex I do this. And as I do it I think of other times that I've killed her:

1. For scarring my favourite doll with a Magic Marker
2. For scouring my patent-leather shoes with sandpaper
3. For making me stick my finger up her dirty anus when we played doctors and nurses
4. For every single time she has called me silly or stupid
5. For telling boys that I fancied them
6. For tearing my velvet coat into a thousand pieces
7. For flirting with my father

136

hope and betrayal

My recurring dream. I am standing by an open window wearing blue, reading a book. Gabriel is standing some distance from me and he's whispering white words. The words drift from his mouth, land at my feet, coil round my body and enter my right ear. I cannot read the words nor hear them. I can feel them in my bloodstream, cross my heart and move downwards to my stomach, where they stay, leaving a sensation of warmth. And then I fall. My knees hard against the cold floor. And he vanishes.

A history of home pregnancy testers. The early ones, delicate arrangements of miniature glass test tubes, perspex boxes and angled mirrors. Complicated instructions. Urinate in a sterilised jar; use supplied pipette to transfer specified number of drops of urine to test tube. In test tube there is already a fine powder. Gently shake test tube until powder dissolves. Place in holder of perspex box. To the test tube add contents of supplied plastic tube. Use scissors to snip top. Wait five minutes. Using angled mirror to see bottom of test tube wait to see if a pink circle forms. If it forms you are pregnant. Results. Rinse everything out. Use test tube and holder as vase for tiny flowers.

Gradual progression: scissors no longer required – the plastic tube has a snap-off top.

Further developments. The holder is redesigned. It is taller, slimmer. The test tube is thinner. The plastic tube of liquid is no longer part of kit. Everything is already in the test tube, just add the number of drops of urine, gently shake and place in holder. Wait for results. The wait time has been reduced to only three minutes. Pregnancy, if you have it, is still a pink circle reflected in the mirror.

Dramatic invention: a magic stick with two windows. Made of grey plastic, it looks like a flat pen. Simple instructions. Remove cap at one end to reveal long thick felt nib. Urinate on this for five seconds only. Replace cap and lay stick on a flat surface. Wait. If you are pregnant a blue line slowly materialises in both windows . . .

140

the chosen one

Lorimer sticks his tongue in my ear. He does this both before and after he comes, as I have asked him to. His tongue is warm and wet, his saliva copious and sticky. I imagine the tiny baby floating down my ear. Visualise his sperm penetrating my egg. Think I can feel it. A sharp little stab. We are going to have five children. Three girls and two boys. The girls will look like me, the boys like him. I see them as identical miniature versions of ourselves. They will walk behind us in single file in descending size. I want to be called Mama. He wants to be called Dad. We will have to buy one of those Japanese people carriers to ferry them to school and back. There will be room enough for the dog, the cat, the hamsters in their cages, the goldfish. Realistically, we know we can afford to have one. Just.

Marriage can come later, but first the children. We light candles and incense and rub each other with jasmine oil. Surround our bed with feasts of bread and cheese, red wine, crisps and humous, beer, lemon sherbets. He wants to take me away but he knows my fear of travelling. We get a duvet cover and sheets printed with the map of the world. We have sex in India, in Africa, in America. And all of the time we seem to be laughing. But each month the cramps in my thighs and stomach tell me before I see the blood that we have failed. We remain optimistic. Keep trying. Think of names. I like Delilah. He likes Helen. It's going to be a girl first. I know it. A year passes and still there is blood instead of a child. So we go to the doctor. He says, 'Don't worry, it can take up to three years – no tests needed yet.'

Thermometers, graphs, hormone testers and cold baths. Sex becomes a perfunctory process. Lorimer and I descend back along the evolutionary trail; reproduction the only purpose of survival. I am not taken to clouds, to castles, to dark forests as I used to be. Our communication reduces to mundane necessity and sexual grunts. But still the blood comes. Twelve months more.

Lorimer is tested. His millions and millions and millions of sperm are healthy and happy. This makes him dance, buoys his libido. He buys me naughty underwear and tight dresses and high heels. A new set of bed linen. Silk. Red. I have blood tests in white-tiled rooms and scans that render my inside parts a black-and-white topological haze. Nothing inside me looks how I have seen it in all my books. 'Do you want a printout?' the nurse asks. I take it and keep it in my wallet. Finally, I am injected with a special dye which shows up any anomalies. There are no clear reasons why my body will not house Lorimer's child. It just will not.

We try IVF. My body is pumped full of hormones. My ovaries produce fifteen eggs. I am harvested. My fifteen eggs are put in a glass with Lorimer's dancing sperm. The results are ten embryos that look as delicate as the microscopic images of snowflakes I remember seeing as a child, as phantom-like and luminescent as the images of deep-sea plankton. Three of these beautiful creatures are placed inside me. The rest are frozen. The wait is a week long.

It does not work. Lorimer walks around the flat slamming doors. Opening and closing cupboards and drawers. I try and joke, lighten the moment.

'You won't find any in there.'

The front door opens and slams closed.

Selina didn't say it but I could sense her relief. I could feel it in the way she held my hand, the tightness of her grip and the way she held me so close to her that I could hardly breathe. 'I'm so sorry,' she said. I didn't believe her. I felt her smile against my neck.

Adele was just Adele. All sympathy and understanding and hope.

All five times the IVF doesn't work. My thick succulent womb does not seem to want to keep hold of the embryos. Lets them go. Lets them disappear with my blood into the sewage systems of London and eventually, I hope, to the sea. I imagine them evaporating into the sky. The clouds, my children. The rain, my children. I cut my hair short so my ears show, pluck my eyebrows into a thin line and take to wearing tight black dresses. To show my body, to mock my body, to grieve. It is a death for which there is no body, no funeral, no memories. It is a bereavement of future rather than past memories. Lorimer hardly talks any more. He spends all his time reading.

Lorimer suggests we use a surrogate. Part of my desire to have a child is to be pregnant; to use the very thing in me that defines my gender. During the times we hoped that I might have conceived I used to put pillows under my T-shirts and walk around the flat looking at myself in all the mirrors.

I am thinking of the features I share with my grandmother. Her hairline, I had been told, her fondness for eating heavily buttered bread sprinkled with white sugar and her propensity for crying when she saw frail elderly men. I have my mother's eyes and hands and ability to finish everything I start. I have my father's legs and temperament. My grandmother, my mother, my sister and myself all have a streak of grey hair at the nape of our necks and get rashes when we eat pineapple.

These are the reasons I don't want another woman's child. I want it to have a history I recognise. It would be different if I found a child, if one just appeared on the doorstep. I would no doubt raise it and love it as my own.

'Enough,' I say to Lorimer and we part without argument.

The sky is stormy black and the beast moves slowly, quietly, carefully through the trees. The beast is stealth. The beast is slime green. Gangrene green. Spring-sap green. The colour green of old oxidised copper. Sometimes It is lion, sometimes dragon, sometimes both. It knows when I am on my own. Sniffs me out, watches me as I walk the path through the forest. Watches me with Its yellow eyes. Eyes as big as saucers. Shiny like mirrors. I can see myself in Its eyes. See myself stand bone-rigid still. Petrified. Stone. But I feel the beat of the ground against my feet, the harshness of breath in my throat, branches pull at clothes and hair, tear skin. I run in a space that feels like for ever. The gaps between the trees whistle by, remind me of blowing out candles on a birthday cake. Hold this light to guide me. Behind me It bellows, roars, rages, grows silent. Follows.

All around, the wind moans. I am in the clearing. I call for Gabriel. I can only call him here. Gabriel cannot fight in the thick of the trees. Needs space for attack. Needs space for escape. The now dragon now lion now two heads now three shows itself. Circles me. I can see myself in Its eyes, my fists in my mouth. Its breath smells of death: sweet and rancid. A high-pitched sound cuts the air. All eyes to the swirling sky. There is Gabriel; diving, plunging, falling, wings folded back, an arm outstretched, in his hand a knife.

The beast is on Its hind legs, as big as two men. Lightning. Gabriel's shadow climbs down the beast's chest. Their bodies slam together. Gabriel jams the knife in all the way to the hilt. Through flesh through muscle through bone. For a moment all is still. And then the beast howls deep from Its belly. Its haunches quiver and It lunges for Gabriel, the blood pouring from Its wound, grabs Gabriel's foot, pulls him down. There is a struggle. Gabriel's wings beat madly against the undergrowth. He walks on his wings, on his back. Feathers. I can see his white hands around the beast's large green neck. His thumbs dig deep in the hollow of Its throat. The beast weakens. Collapses on to Its side. Dies with Its eyes open. A sea of blood bleeds out, seeps into the ground and in between Gabriel's sandalled toes. Washes away in the rain that hammers down. Me under the shelter of Gabriel's wing, we watch the beast's skin turn darkest black. Watch ourselves in Its eyes.

Significant things Selina has done in the seven years Lorimer and I have been trying for a baby:

1987: Selina went for an Aids test. She is negative.

1988: Selina learnt to drive; she passed first time. This pleases her. I still cannot drive.

1988: Selina bought a lime-green tie-dyed hooded top and went to her first rave. She took ecstasy. She did not take it again. She said it made her want to talk about things she doesn't want to talk about.

1989: Selina made a pass at Lorimer. Lorimer said he declined.

1990: Selina learnt how to use a computer (Quark Express, Photoshop). She thinks she has found her vocation. She does flyers for clubs and leaflets and business cards. She bought a car. A vintage pink Saab. It breaks down all the time. She met Eric. Almost seemed serious: he moved in with her for five months.

1991: She resents turning thirty. I know she does not want to admit that she is thirty. She spends money on beauty products.

1992: Selina gets her nose pierced.

We meet at the Goose and Crown in Camden in Delancey Street. We order a bottle of white wine and a basket of bread. It comes with olive oil. I wear a black dress, loafers, and my hair is short. I look smart. She is queen of grunge. She wears cycling shorts, big boots, two T-shirts, one worn over the other. Her colour scheme: khaki, grey and black. She has been tempted to dread her hair; Adele told me she talked her out of it. Her hair stays thick and brown and curly. She wears it long. She wears it now in a centre parting. Like she used to.

'It is sad, so close to your seventh anniversary.' I was not aware she was following the dates so closely. 'But longer than most marriages,' she adds. She smiles. 'I saw him yesterday, at Adele's – he seemed OK.' She's careful not to mention his name. She dips her bread in the olive oil and sprinkles on some salt. I do the same.

'Are you going to move back with me?' Her smile is hopeful.

'No, but thank you,' I say. I say it gently, quietly.

She drinks another glass of wine. She looks me up and down.

'You're starting to look boring,' she says.

'I don't like your hair short,' she says.

I pour myself another glass of wine. I want her to shut up. I use the napkin to wipe my eyes.

'It's grown quite a lot,' I say.

'It's still too short,' she says.

'At least I brush mine.'

This makes Selina laugh. We both chew on another piece of bread. View the gathering lunchtime crowd.

'Last night I went clubbing with Kate.' She now refers to my sister by name.

'I know,' I say. Kate rang me and told me. Selina danced all night. I asked Kate how Selina dances. She still undulates.

Selina watches me over the top of her glass. She smiles.

'Drink up, I want to take you somewhere,' she says.

She opens her bags and produces a mirror and lipstick. She reapplies it carefully while I pay the bill. She is grunge. But she has not lost the make-up.

Half an hour later, in her nose and in my nose, a gold stud. She took me to a tattoo parlour near the Camden Lock Bridge. We now each have a pierced nose. It was her gift to me, she said.

Lorimer met someone else very quickly and within a year there is a child. I feel no animosity. I ask him to send me a photograph but he says that would be cruel.

'I don't love you any more,' I say. 'I'm just curious.'

I carry the picture around with me in my wallet. I have been tempted from time to time to pretend she's mine. She doesn't look like Lorimer at all.

Every other Saturday night Selina works.

Afterwards she goes clubbing.

Before she leaves, she rings me (as she does on Fridays).

Always the same conversation:

'Wanna come?'

'No, thanks.'

'Sure?'

'Sure.'

'Laters, then.'

On Mondays and Thursdays Selina comes to the studio in the late afternoon, when she has finished in the restaurant, and waits for me.

Our weekly timetable:

Monday: cinema.

Tuesday: Selina's flat. Takeaway. Watch a video.

Wednesday: Selina works. I do accounts at studio.

Thursday: meal – the rota: French, Italian, Chinese, Indian, fish and chips.

Friday: Selina works. I visit old college friends.

Saturday: 8 p.m. – meet Adele in a bar in Camden or Islington or Soho.

Sunday: 1 p.m. – Adele's for lunch. Selina picks me up in her car.

In two years, she never asked if I missed Lorimer; she talked about my hair.

How much better I looked when it again covered my ears. How nice it was to see it again shoulder-length.

May 1994. Dawn. My studio. I tell Selina what I do to her when I am angry with her. She holds her head protectively in her hands.

I list my account . . .

8. For whispering dirty things in Lorimer's ear.
9. For touching his cock.
10. For spilling red wine all over the dress: it has taken me all night to finish the dress.

Selina moves her hands away from her head. She looks up at me. Selina is suddenly sober. She tells me Lorimer 'fucked' her every day in the month of June. As if this makes any difference.

'I could see roses from the window.' This lets me know they had done it in our bed, while we were still together. Before he moved out.

At the door she hesitated, threw me a look over her shoulder.

She had come to see me because she had things she needed to tell me. Serious things she needed to talk about, a bottle in her hand. 'Get a glass, Mads.' Her words slurred. That discussion never started; she spilt the wine, she smiled stupidly, there was no apology. I told her what I did when I was angry with her.

11. For having sex with Lorimer.

We have not spoken for a year. There has been no contact. No postcards. No letters. No phone calls. No birthday card. No Christmas card.

I have bundled together all photographs of her or us and put them in an envelope in the bottom drawer of my wardrobe, right at the back.

I have collected all souvenirs of her and put them in a shoebox and written her name on it and stored them next to the photographs.

Things about her that haunt me: Her crooked little finger. Her chipped front tooth. The way that one side of her mouth goes up more than the other when she smiles. The silvery stretch marks that lace the skin on her belly.

part two

messengers

I thread the needle. The paper patterns I have already tacked on guide me. Each seed pearl needs three stitches to keep it in place. The stitches must be neat and even. The knot invisible. There are still over a hundred to sew on. In the shape of small flowers. It is not a labour to do it. I enjoy doing it. It gives me pleasure. It is like meditation. It keeps me distracted from the fact that I am flying. That I am travelling. It protects me from the type of thoughts that looking at clouds can bring: nostalgic thoughts. Selina thoughts. I count the stitches as I do them. I don't think Adele would like me sewing Selina thoughts into her wedding veil.

We only refer to her as 'S'. As if mentioning her name is a dangerous thing to do. 'S' returned the invitation with 'too busy' scrawled across it. Angry writing. Big capital letters. An exclamation mark at the end. 'S' still sees Lorimer; is a family friend now, I am told. Whatever that means. She gave Adele a choice, me, or her. Adele refuses to choose, so 'S' no longer returns her calls. I haven't told her the reason we are not talking. If she knows she pretends she doesn't. She is good at that.

There will be a thousand white roses and 150 doves in a hill town on the outskirts of Florence.

Florence is spelt Firenze in Italian. Flowers are spelt fiori.

The train from Pisa takes an hour. I say his name as I do the stitches. It seems appropriate. Break it up into its syllables. One for each stitch. Gabriel. There are still ten pearls left as the train pulls into Firenze station.

Adele is on the platform waiting for me. Blonde and shiny. The collar of her cream raincoat turned up. Her handbag held by its strap with both hands carefully positioned in front of her knees. Her back straight. Head up. Looking like she always does, as if she may at any moment be photographed.

'*Ciao, bella,*' she says as she hugs me.

'Hello,' I whisper back.

In my hotel room I sew the remaining pearls on as she stands. The veil covers her from head to foot. Makes her disappear. I asked her to put it on after she showed me the card. It says: 'Have a lovely day – love and kisses, Selina'. I said nothing. I take my time. Give each pearl six stitches. Adele is busy making phone calls from under the veil even though she told me in the taxi that she had ticked off everything on her checklist. Had listed everything to me again. Making phone calls is her way of keeping calm. She told me this once. She takes the veil off so I can steam out the creases. She sits on the end of my bed and reads my guidebook, talks about what Claudio, her husband-to-be, will be wearing, suggests I go to the café at the Boboli Gardens if I want to take 'some fucking brilliant photographs'. Her voice is PR-trained; she gives nothing away but I know she is still upset: she is stroking her nose with her little finger. She works from the bridge down. Sometimes she is covering an eye with her hand, sometimes her mouth. She can't join me. She has a manicure appointment. She shows me the nail varnish she has chosen. She says it has taken her weeks to find one to match the colour and lustre

160

of the pearls. I wrap the veil ready for her to take. My peace offering: I let her paint my nails as she waits for her cab.

We part outside the hotel. It is raining. Adele puts her hand out to feel it. She smiles. Adele can find a smile for everything. 'Hope it doesn't do this tomorrow,' she says.

She points me in the direction of the Uffizi. I know where it is. I have known for twenty years. I made sure that my hotel would be less than a five-minute walk away. She is already in the taxi and on her mobile phone. Speaking Italian very fast. She waves goodbye and rolls up the window.

I join the throng of groups of day trippers and tourists. Walk the short distance along the riverfront.

The queue is 500-deep; at least. It inches slowly forward. I wait patiently. It seems right somehow to have to wait. More romantic. More devoted.

the painting

The colours in the painting have more depth, more vibrancy, the pinks are pinker than I remember. But the picture is the same.

Gabriel is kneeling on his right knee. He holds a white lily in his left hand and his right hand is outstretched to Mary. Mary is standing near a lectern that holds her open book. She holds both her arms out towards Gabriel. Beyond them the view from the window is as it has always been. Immediately outside, the tall delicate ash tree, behind it the curve of the river, a boat and a bridge, on either side green fields, and at the back on the left the castle with its spires on the hill. Everything looks quiet and serene.

Everything is how it should be. Every fold of Gabriel's pink robe, the half-close of his pale yellow wings, the hold of Mary's hands, the placement of each of her fingers in the air, how their eyes look to each other's raised hands. His intently, hers shyly.

Her eyes look to his hand; his eyes look to her hand. I still can't tell if she is moving towards him or pulling away from him. If she is reaching out to touch his hand and meet his body for the first time or if they have just separated for the last time and, with her eyes cast down to his hand, she moves away. There is a tenderness between them, a concern in their eyes, a softness of expression as if trying to understand the moment and each other.

His eyes look to her hand; her eyes look to his hand.

Everything in the picture focuses the viewer's eye to the space between their hands. All the desire and pain between them is caught there.

I notice for the first time that the forefinger of Gabriel's hand rests on the same plane as the edge of the window, as if he has pushed the wall aside to make the window and reveal the world beyond. Behind him is the distant view; behind her is only the dark grey wall of her room. He offers her the world, offers to take her from her books and solitude. If she touches his hand she will go outside. And the way she stands she looks unsteady as if she is just about to fall at his feet. The bend of her knee as it collapses beneath her blue gown catches the light.

I am the only customer at the café. I sit outside under a large umbrella. I take pictures of the panoramic view making sure to place the golden globe of the Duomo to the left of frame. I do another set of pictures scanning across with small over-laps so I can stick them together later and get what I am seeing. I take a picture of the sky thick with steel clouds. I take a picture of my cup of coffee, full and empty. I ask the waitress to take a picture of me with the city in the back-ground. My pose: plaintive with cigarette.

It has stopped raining but the gardens are still deserted. It is deathly quiet and still. That sort of damp quiet as if the wet earth and wood have sucked up all the sound in the world. There does not even seem to be any birdsong. The air feels thick as if you could hold it.

I wander down one of the long sloping avenues, mean-dering left and right through the specially cultivated tunnels of shrubs which run along each side. Now and then they lead into lush squares of grass, each with a solitary white statue at its centre and benches placed evenly around the perimeter. I work my way around the perimeter paths to another tunnel, weave my way back to the avenue and follow it down. I am grateful when I see and hear a bird fly across my path.

At the end of the avenue is a large wrought-iron gate. I go through a smaller gate built into the large gate and find myself in a circular courtyard that is built around a circular pond. The courtyard is full of pots of miniature orange and lemon trees. The fruit pulls heavily at the branches and as I watch a lemon falls plopping into the water, the ripples making all the other oranges and lemons that already float there bob gently up and down. I watch as the water returns to a mirror still. In it I can see the sky darken. The silence seems for a moment to deepen then is broken; it has started to rain again. It pats gently on the leaves and water. I take a photograph and then walk through to the other side of the courtyard to another gate that leads down to a main road. I take a taxi back to the hotel. Sleep.

the wedding party

It is all going according to Adele's plan. The sun is shining; the sky is blue. On the raised platform by the dance floor, under some trees, a quartet plays Vivaldi's *Four Seasons*. The chairs and swinging sofas have been arranged in groups of three on the grass and in case it rains there is the marquee. The fountain has been filled with new goldfish. The buffet tables, set up at each end of the patio – in order to avoid a crush – are laid with a dainty feast.

There are: Smoked Trout & Cucumber Filo Tartlets, Herbed Brioche Sandwiches, Prawn and Cucumber Hearts with Sweet Chilli Sauce, Cheddar Crackers with Goat's Cheese, Tomatoes and Basil, Mixed Bruschetta Platter, Brioche filled with Wild Mushrooms, Quail Egg & Smoked Salmon Tartlets, Saffron Mussels in Garlic Bread, Caviar Eclairs, Elderflower Jellies, Summer Berry Tartlets, Vanilla Shortbreads with Fromage Frais and Lime Curd, Individual Chocolate-Covered Heart Cakes, decorated with an individual Rose, companions to the larger Heart-Shaped Chocolate-Covered Wedding Cake, sprinkled with Pink and White Rose Petals. There is Jasmine Infusion for those not drinking champagne, all served in glasses hand-painted in silver.

It is all very glamorous. Very tasteful. It is magazine material.

For over six months I have listened to Adele recite the menu.

167

I am tempted to count how many items there are of each food: Adele says with a finger buffet you have to allow eight to twelve substantial items per person. More if the guests are to last the whole day. I run through the food items again. I run through all the various objects in their various places again. I take comfort in checking Adele's checklist: of the 250 guests I know only three: Lorimer and his mother and his father and they seem to be avoiding me. The guests have already divided, subdivided into their known groups. The children have found each other, formed a gang. Ringleaders have been established. They vie for supremacy of the bouncy castle that has been specially made to match the marquee. They have made the marquee their headquarters.

The waitresses smile at me each time I take another glass of champagne, as if they are counting. I take my third glass, smile nervously at the crowd of strangers in case anyone should be watching, which they aren't. Wish that the drink would get to my head quicker. There is a man with a very tiny video camera recording the guests. Hired on instruction that he must be discreet as possible. Or so Adele had said. He mingles as quietly as he can. I follow his moves. Among the Italians there's a lot of embracing and kissing, heated conversation and big gestures. I half expect subtitles.

I survey the other females. I worry that the faux fur I have put around the collar and cuffs of my jacket are too over the top; that the coral pink shoes are too high and too bright; that the hat is too big.

The women from Adele's PR office wear expensive shift dresses and contrasting jackets of the same length. They all wear a little silver pendant on a chain. Or a torque. They look like they have bought a job lot on the hats, and on their highlights. They look like they have shared their make-up. It is the sort of make-up that doesn't look like any is being worn. It is the natural look. My lipstick is bright red.

The other women, the Italian women, both young and old, are dressed in suits. There are at least five Chanel suits. Most wear scarves, brightly patterned silk, tied or pinned at the neck, or chiffon, long and floaty, which drape over a shoulder and catch the wind. They all have impeccable nails, painted in shades that match their lipsticks. Their shoes are beige or camel-coloured. There is a slight sheen to their legs. Their handbags are quilted, with gilt chain straps and loud emblem buckles. All their hair is coiffeured.

No one else is wearing plaits. No one else is wearing faux fur.

All the men wear frock coats and cravats. Apart from Adele's father who wears the clan kilt. Lorimer, of course, wears his shirt open, no cravat. His wife and mother, his little girl running in and out of his legs, flank him. His wife is dressed in a sophisticated suit. No doubt under strict instruction from Adele. His mother is dressed to stand out: a fitted polka-dot dress, white on black, full skirt to just below the knee. I note that it has been well made. Well tailored. A large white hat with a black sash, and huge dark sunglasses, which cover a third of her face, finishes off the outfit. She looks like an ageing, but still beautiful fifties Italian film star. Lorimer's father comes to join them as I watch, then comes Adele. I made her her dress as a gift. It is ivory crêpe. Simple. Bias-cut, high neck, medieval sleeves. It clings tight to all of her slim tall frame. It is trimmed with seed pearls in the shape of small flowers. There are shoes to match. She wears her hair high, adorned with a tiara. Her veil now slung over a shoulder. Claudio, the groom, dressed in silver grey and cream, comes to stand beside her. In the background, low hills and blue sky.

The photographer slightly rearranges their grouping and takes the photograph.

It is three years since I have seen Lorimer. He looks a little fatter, a little older. His hairline has receded, there is grey at his temples.

All members of the clan see me and raise their chins in acknowledgement and smile – a family habit – but no one comes over to say hello.

The photographer looks at his list and starts to call names. Women get out their compacts and lipsticks in preparation. I do the same, try to integrate. My name is called. Adele puts her arm around me. I ask her about the faux fur. I think she's more concerned with the plaits. Lorimer and his wife watch me. The photograph is taken. As I leave the stand, Selina's name is called. Adele makes an irritated waving gesture to the photographer to call the next name and Lorimer catches my eye. He gives me a strange, sad, smile, but then turns to talk to his wife.

I try to talk to the group of PR women. They keep to themselves. Their skills do not extend to languages or socialising with strangers, including me. Two of them comment on Adele's dress. They say it is 'fantastic' and 'gorgeous' and 'divine'. They both use these identical words to describe it even though one has heard the other say them.

They must have had a meeting, taken pity on me. They smile as they approach and suddenly they surround me en masse: mother, father, Lorimer, his wife, their child. There is the necessary introduction to the child, who I have difficulty looking at, and wife, who smiles at me too much, and who I don't think should have kissed me. Lorimer seems uncertain whether to kiss me. I save him the decision. I shake his hand. There is an awkward polite exchange regarding health, weather and the quality of wedding, which, everyone agrees, is very fine. And then they are gone again as quickly as they appeared. 'To do the rounds,' the father says. Lorimer hangs back a moment longer, as if he has something else to say. He begins as if to say it. Seems to change his mind. 'I'll catch you later,' he says, and he is gone.

I wander around on my own, make large circles, attempt to look like I am going somewhere or about to join someone. I keep a smile ready for those who catch my eye. Namely Adele. Alternately I wish that Selina was here and am glad that she is not. I consider loosening my plaits. Question why I didn't make the faux fur detachable. Smoke too many cigarettes. Eat. Get drunk. Watch Lorimer. Wait for him to be on his own so I can go and ask him what he wanted to tell me. But he is never on his own. I give up. I settle in to a chair near the dance floor and watch the crooner do Frank Sinatra cover songs.

After the speeches an accordion leads the first dance. Adele and Claudio take to the floor. They take their positions. Hold each other close. Adele makes three little nods with her head and they begin. The dancing lessons have paid off. In dappled light they circle the expanse of floor in a graceful sweeping waltz all the time smiling at each other. The guests love it: they clap and whoop and stamp their feet, till the accordion can't be heard at all. As they circle the floor for the third time the 150 doves are released into the air above them. All the women simultaneously gasp and tears run down their cheeks. I wipe my face with the back of my hand.

Someone is talking to me; it is Lorimer.

'Maddy – do you want to go for a walk?' he says.

I look up at him.

'Thank God for that – I thought you were going to ask me to dance.'

Out of the corner of my eye I see at a distance his wife and mother watching us. His wife urges him on with her hand.

Lorimer puts his hand on my back. He guides me away from the party, into the house, up the stairs and into Claudio's father's study. He closes the door.

He says I have to promise not to tell Adele. I know by the softness of his voice that it is something serious. His voice and that he seems not to know what to do with his hands. Whether he should touch me or not. He takes my hand and then lets go of it, puts his hand in his jacket pocket as if he is looking for something and then takes it out again. He studies the floor for a moment and then he looks at me and takes a deep breath, begins to speak. He speaks slowly, as if reciting dictation: Selina wants me to know that she is sick; she wants me to know all the details: the cancer started in the bowel, it has now spread to the spleen, to the pancreas, to the liver. End of message.

Cold. Precise. Clinical. As he mentioned each organ I located it in the human body. Visualised it. Made a picture. She knew I would do this. A habit of mine to place things. I smile when I know I shouldn't, nearly laugh: this is Selina being affectionate. This is Selina being kind to be cruel. I cover my mouth with my hand to hide my smile.

Lorimer is staring at me. I am thinking about why people always say that they have an illness when in fact it has them. I am waiting for the air in the room to still. For my heart to plummet. I am waiting to react. Nothing happens. I remain calm and collected. I light a cigarette. Inhale deeply. Flick the ash into my hand. Am very aware of its small warmth. I say nothing as I walk around the room. The spaces between things look suddenly more defined. Things more themselves. The vase on the window sill more vase-like. The sofa more sofa-like. Lorimer sitting on it, his eyes following me, looking concerned but not knowing what else to say, has a weight and solidity about him as if he is cast in stone. I try to imagine what the cancer looks like. I imagine it looks gnarled like a walnut, but black and with a texture like gristle. Her body is ripe with walnuts.

I focus on the laughter and noise coming up from outside. I go to the window. I pour the ash and cigarette into the vase. It hisses out in the tiny layer of water at the bottom. Through the window I can see that the other guests have joined Adele and Claudio on the dance floor. The band is doing a cheesy version of Abba's 'Waterloo'. Jackets have been removed, skirts hitched up. I make my way to the door, announce that I am going back to the party. Lorimer follows me out telling me he will break the news to Adele once she is back from her honeymoon. 'She will take it badly,' he says. 'Yes,' is all I say. I think he is telling me I am not but cannot be bothered to argue. His wife is waiting at the bottom of the stairs. She stands when she hears us, smiles at me in a sympathetic way. I do not smile back. I see Lorimer make a patting motion towards the floor. She stays where she is.

Lorimer stays and sits with me, plies me with drink. He informs me that Selina insisted I be told today. At the wedding. In person, by him. He had wanted to tell me before, but she had made him promise not to. His wife could vouch for him if need be. His wife is lingering close by, keeping a guarded eye. I smile at her. She smiles back. And I still have to ask him. To be sure. Did he sleep with Selina? He says, 'Yes, once.' But it was in her bed, not ours. There were no roses. As if this makes any difference. His wife has taken my smile as an invitation. She has joined us just in time to get the gist of the conversation. There is an awkward silence. An exchange of looks and she is off and Lorimer is chasing after her. I watch them argue at the side of the marquee.

It is getting dark. A heavy bass beat suddenly fills the air. Gets right under the skin. Right to the heart. The DJ has put on the techno. He pushes it up to full volume. Coloured-light and oil projections pour across the dancers. Adele comes to get me and drags me on to the dance floor.

the seduction

Selina used to say if you want to seduce a man, ask him for a light, touch his hand as he lights the cigarette, look deep into his eyes, take a drag of the cigarette, smile sweetly, blow the smoke up, not into his face.

He had been sitting on his own while everyone else seemed to be dancing. I'd seen him earlier watching me talking to Lorimer. I thought maybe he was going to come and talk to me when I was on my own, but he didn't. He just watched me, no smile, but a knowing look, as if he was waiting for me to come to him. So I went to him. Unlit cigarette ready in my hand, poised. I lent forward, waited. He said nothing, just stared at me as he brought the light to my face. I made sure to touch his hand as I shielded the flame. Kept my eyes on his the whole time. Pale blue eyes. Cold hands. I blew the smoke up into the sky. And then I went away again.

He said nothing, just stared at me. I moved on to the dance floor. Glanced at him over my shoulder to make sure he was still watching. Smiled. He didn't smile. He just looked at me in his knowing way. I let him watch me dance. Had another drink. All night I just let him watch me. At the end of the night I went back over to him. He said nothing again, but stood, followed me, took my hand.

'Your place or mine?' he said.

He tells me his name. Roberto. Apart from that he hardly speaks. He is a cousin of Claudio's. Adele has talked about

177

him sometimes. She calls him 'serious, mysterious', but this is what attracted me to him.

In the morning all my clothes are still on, except my shoes, and I have been tucked in. The sheets tight. Swaddled. And Roberto is watching me from the armchair.

'Hello,' I say, and he comes and sits beside me. He doesn't smile.

There is a bruise, small and dark purple, about the size of a penny in the middle of his cheek. He says I kicked him when he took off my shoe. He says it doesn't hurt. He had to put me to bed because I passed out.

'Sorry,' I say, and reassure him that I'm fine now and swing my legs round to get up, but am unable to stand. I lie back down, stare at the ceiling, try to keep very still.

'Sick?' he says.

'Yes,' I say.

'Too much drink?' he says.

'No,' I say, and ask him to call a doctor.

Even in Italian he seems to say very little. On the phone his instructions seem to be short and sharp. Economical.

The doctor confirms what I know. He shines his special torch in my ears. 'Very bad,' he says. 'It could take a week to clear,' he says, and then he leaves.

Roberto makes another phone call.

I need to go again. Before, Roberto had called a girl from reception to help me. But she has gone to lunch. He leans me against the wall of the bathroom and starts to leave.

'Please,' I say, 'you're going to have to help me.'

He doesn't seem to understand at first. And when he does, he is not sure whether to be angry or embarrassed. Without looking, he puts his cold hands up my dress, pulls my pants to my knees, and sits me on the toilet. He turns on the tap for my benefit and leaves the room but leaves the door open. He sits on the corner of the bed watching me. He picks up the drawing the doctor has done for me. More for Roberto, who thought perhaps that he has done this to me, even though I have tried to explain to him that I'd had it before. The drawing shows the spiral of the inner ear. The doctor has flecked the drawing with tiny marks to show Roberto the effects of the virus, how it paralyses the hairs and affects the balance; how it makes me fall down.

Roberto helps me back to bed. Feeds me the pills the doctor has left to lessen the nausea and the dizziness. I think he hopes this will mean he won't have to help me in the bathroom again. I say, 'Thank you,' and smile. He looks serious, but calm somehow. He makes me think of priests. He says he has nothing better to do. He has taken the week off for the wedding. He has already arranged for his things to be brought from his hotel to mine. In silence, he undresses me, washes my face, runs his hand up the length of my leg. He gives me a look that suggests the night before. 'Later, perhaps,' I say.

We did it in the hotel lift. There had been no talking. Except one question as he touched my back. 'Are your hands always so cold?' I had thought of Selina. Made so much noise that he had to put his hand over my mouth. When we got out of the lift I passed out. 'Just like that,' Roberto tells me, not smiling, and clicking his fingers to demonstrate the moment.

All day he waits for a sign. Any sign that we'll be doing it again. He brushes my hair and then he lies down beside me, on top of the bedclothes, keeping a distance, watching me, not saying a word.

Later that afternoon, again the question, 'Why are your

179

hands always so cold?' as he slips his fingers under the sheets.

I am fine as long as I am horizontal.

For the next four days he doesn't leave the room. He gets up now and then and dresses to accept room service. I like this. I like to watch him undress again.

The floor clutters with trays and newspapers and magazines. Discarded empty crisp and cigarette packets. We keep the shutters closed. The television on all day, the volume low. One afternoon, an Elvis Presley film. *Jailhouse Rock*. Roberto knows all the words. Undoes the buttons on his shirt, pulls the collar over his jacket, quiffs his hair. He seems to sing more than he talks.

The phone rings for the first time. We let it ring for a long time before answering, just staring at its vague shape in the dim room.

It is Selina's mother on the phone. Selina wants to know where I am.

I give Roberto my phone number as we part at Florence station. Watch him put it in his pocket. Know and am not upset that he will never ring.

part three

waiting for selina

The hospital visitors' waiting room is on the eleventh floor. There is a view right across London. It is grey and still and flat: the heat haze has eaten up all the space between things. The sky is so grey-white that it looks as if it has been forgotten. No sound travels up.

The room is full of telly noise; cartoons; Selina's brother is laughing at *Road Runner*. It is like being in a family sitting room, but it isn't.

'She's been asking for you again,' says Selina's mother when I come in, in such a way that I have to say 'Sorry'. Her body looks stiff, although she tries to sit casually on the arm of the sofa, one hand on her lap, the other teasing at Selina's brother's hair. She pretends to watch the telly. Selina's brother nodded at me in the way he does when he doesn't want to talk about what is going on and went straight back to watching the cartoons. His wife sits on the other side of the room flicking through a magazine. She looked up for a moment when I came in, smiled and then carried on flicking. Their son lies on the floor playing a computer game on his GameBoy. He takes no notice of me.

Selina's mother pours brandy into a mug and sips at it. She sees me watching her and offers me the bottle. I shake my head. She looks tired. Her eyes are dark and swollen. Bloodshot. She looks as if she hasn't slept for weeks. All her nights spent crying. I saw her look like this once before,

183

many years ago. She drank gin then. I liked the smell of it. Like perfume and medicine. For months every room of her house had smelt of it, except Selina's room.

I announce that I'm going to check on Selina. They all look up and say 'OK' simultaneously. As I'm leaving the room the boy sighs loudly, rolls on to his back and slaps his head. He looks up at me as I walk past him, says, 'Me stupid, me . . .' His mother quickly kicks his foot to shut him up. On the small screen of his GameBoy flash the words 'game over'.

Selina is sleeping. The nurse said it was best not to disturb her. I watch her from the doorway. She lies on her back; she has forced an arm and leg out from the sheet because it is so hot. Her hand dangles over the edge of the bed. She is wearing her old light blue pyjamas. On the leg that is outside the sheet they have rolled up to her knee.

She is very thin. I can see her skeleton. I listen to her shallow breaths.

I sit on the chair beside the bed. I label the bones I can see outlined under the sheet, through her pyjamas, under her skin. From toe to head I name them, mentally locate them in myself. Phalanges, Metatarsals, Tarsus, Fibula, Tibia, Patella, Femur, Pelvis, Ilium, Sacrum, Ribs, Sternum, Clavicle, Skull. The human skull is made up of twenty-two bones. I can only remember the Mandible. I go down her arm – Humerus, Radius, Ulna, Carpus. Her hand: Metacarpals, Phalanges. I take her hand. It is hot, the palm sweaty. It offers no reflex to my touch. I look at her face. There is sleep dust in the corner of her right eye. Her gold nose stud is still in place. I instinctively search out mine. Her mouth is closed tight and pinched like she is fighting something in her dreams. I stroke her fingers. No one has cleaned her nails.

184

Selina hates having dirty fingernails. This gives me a perverse pleasure.

I watch Selina sleep. I have never watched her sleep. Not face on. She twitches. She mutters things I don't understand. She flares her nostrils wide. She grinds her teeth. When I stayed at her house as children her grinding teeth would wake me. She always slept with her back to me. Her face turned to the wall. My arm pulled over her waist.

I want her to wake up.

I want her to see what I have bought her.

I have bought her things she likes: blue delphiniums, white chocolate, glossy magazines, lavender oil, a Walkman, the best hits of reggae.

I lay everything out on the table at the end of the bed.

I need to get a coffee to keep me awake while Selina sleeps.

I follow the blue line on the floor. Sometimes another line appears; first a red one and then a green one, and I think, perhaps I should follow them for a while, but I don't. I keep to the blue line. A passing doctor said if I follow the blue line I will get back to the ward I want. So I follow the blue line down the empty corridor, round the corner into another corridor that looks exactly like the last; dirty white walls, fluorescent-lit, lots of closed doors, no windows. The last time I saw outside there was a mist over London. It had rained all night but the weather forecast had said it was going to be hot today. It is early morning. Everything is very quiet. Everyone is sleeping.

I keep following the blue line. It takes me from one corridor to the next. Occasionally, the corridors end at a swing door, open out into a larger space, a waiting room full of empty chairs, sometimes a window that looks only into the vacant middle of the building. The blue line goes past the empty chairs to another set of swing doors and another corridor. The blue line takes me from one corridor to the next. I keep walking. Keep turning the corners. Keep following the line. I hear voices, faint, and then coming closer. As I turn into another corridor a group of young student doctors hurry past talking among themselves, their white coats billowing out around them. And then they are gone. The blue line and I are on our own again. I keep close to it, swing the corners with it into its next stretch of lino. The further I go the more desolate and quiet it seems to become. I can hear my breath. I am disappearing. I am floating away cell by cell as I walk. I stop and take a sip of the coffee. It is almost cold now. I drain the cup and put the empty plastic beaker on the line and keep walking. I see a door that has Toilet written on it and go in.

I go to put on some make-up. The light is not flattering and the mirrors too clean. But I am definitely here. I can see every open pore, every stray hair, every evidence of de-elasticising. I put my hands on my cheekbones and pull up. The only significant difference is it makes my mouth look an inch wider and flatter. I let go and watch the skin not spring back. When Selina and I were teenagers we used to think twenty was old. That at thirty we would need walking sticks. My joke: she was older than me. She'd need a stick before me. She said she would use it to hit me. To trip me up. Her joke. Touché. Sword fights in the street. She has just turned thirty-four. I put on my lipstick and brush my hair, smooth my eyebrows.

I carry on following the blue line because this is what I have been told to do. I let myself be led by it. Trust myself entirely to it. For a section of the floor, it suddenly vanishes and a wave of dizziness hits me and makes it seem as if the floor is collapsing beneath me. I have to walk with my hand against the wall to guide me. But the feeling passes as the line appears again just ahead of me. I walk on now as if it were a tightrope, slowly, one foot in front of the other, arms out by my side. The blue line lives up to its promise. Eventually I get to where I need to be: Selina's room. The door is open. She is awake now. She does not smile when she sees me. She pulls out clumps of her hair and drops them on to me. She asks me if I'll shave her head.

rapunzel

The doctors said she could go home. If she wanted. And she did want; now I was here. Now I was home. 'I want to go home.' Her voice clear, sharp. No longer woolly. That had been the drugs. A month's supply of liquid food was loaded into her mother's car. (Selina had said the flavours with a mocking smile – 'strawberry, banana, vanilla and chocolate' – and her mother added, very sincerely, how nice they are, especially when served in a tall glass with ice. Selina looked at her. 'Yes, that really does the trick.' Deadpan.) Next to the liquid food, the large box of various pills. Selina and I sat in the back. I put my arm round her but she asked me to move over because she felt claustrophobic. All the windows had to be opened. She didn't want to talk. She felt sick. She leant her head out of the window. When our childhood streets came into view she took my hand, but didn't look at me.

Her old room was ready. Fresh sheets, the curtains cleaned, a big bunch of flowers. Her mother listed them as she walked around the room, touching each one as she spoke. She unpacked her daughter's things. Selina stayed outside on the landing. She had wanted to go home to her flat. They had fought about it at the hospital. Her mother said it would be easier if she stayed with her. 'It's for the best,' she said as she left the room and went downstairs. Next door my mother was finishing making me up a bed. That was the condition: if she went home, so would I.

We went out into the garden. Her mother set up the chair and parasol; she brought me a towel, scissors, Selina's father's old electric shaver, a fresh set of batteries.

I start at the nape of her neck. I move steadily towards the crown with even sweeps. I work in sections across her head from right to left. Underneath her hair, the skin of her head is a delicate waxy white.

We don't speak. She winces every now and then when I push the shaver too hard against her skull. Tuts and whines my name or shifts awkwardly in the seat because of the pain in her lower back.

She said it seemed appropriate for me to do it. Didn't want anyone else to do it. I had said that I'd shave my head too. If she wanted. She said I was being childish; said that it was her illness. Hers. Not mine.

Her mother watches us from the kitchen window. She calls out; tells me to make sure Selina keeps in the shade. I readjust the parasol. Selina readjusts the chemo-release gadget that is strapped to her waist. Every so often it whirrs and trickles its stuff through tubes to a hole in her chest.

Buried or burnt. Her mother has asked me to find out what she would prefer; she has to think ahead, she has to make plans. She was strict and stern as she spoke. I reminded her that the doctors had said there was still some chance of recovery. She made a tiny space between her finger and thumb and shook her head and walked away. If I ask, it will be like I am saying to her she is going to die. It is not something I dare to suggest to her. That she may die. She may never talk to me again.

A large bead of sweat has collected in the dip at the base of her skull; I wipe it away with my fingers. She leans her head to one side because it tickles. I tell her to keep still.

On her lap is a plait of her hair. She made me plait it first, what remained of it, and then cut the plait off before shaving her head. As a keepsake. For her mother. She fiddles with it, drags it back and forth across her thighs, strokes the bound end of it against her bare knee, runs it up her arm to the crook of her elbow. Draws circles with it. Something she is thinking about is making her smile. She clears her throat to speak.

'Lorimer,' she says, 'how is he?' Her voice is low and a bit husky, the way she makes it when she wants to be suggestive.

She cranes her neck round to me.

'Does he still wear his shirts so you can slip your hand inside?' She grins at me. Shows me her teeth. She stares at me. Waits.

I push just a little harder with the shaver. Enough to nip her shiny scalp. She brings her hand to her head, examines the tiny speck of blood on her finger. She seems pleased. She smiles at me and turns away, nodding her head as if I have fulfilled my brief.

I finish. I brush the hair off her shoulders. I bring her a mirror and her red lipstick. She puts her hand over her face with the initial shock, looks through her fingers. She takes a deep breath, takes away her hand and then she admires herself. She turns her head this way and that and runs her hand over it. She applies the lipstick carefully, using her little finger to tidy it to the outline of her mouth. She smudges the residue on to the outer edge of each of her eyes, just under the brow. As she does all this I stand behind her. For a second the reflection of the two of us is caught. Her face, long, thin, gaunt, like someone has grabbed her skin and pegged it tight behind her head. Her eyes as big as eggs now she has no hair. My face next to hers like someone has taken a bicycle pump to it; pumped it as round as the moon. She gives me a faint smile. She gives me the mirror and lipstick and tells me to put some on. So I put on the lipstick. She brings her little finger to my mouth and tidies the outline. She wipes what is left on her finger on to my eyes.

I pass her the wig that the hospital has given her. She has chosen a blonde one. The blonde is like mine. The style: straight, shoulder-length with a fringe, the way I wear it.

She takes the mirror from me. She looks at herself.

'It doesn't suit you,' I say.

She looks at herself a little longer and then drags the wig off her head and throws it on to the grass. It lands upside down. It looks like some rare breed of dog lying on its back waiting for its stomach to be rubbed. We both stare at it. I have been scalped. I prod at it with my foot, pick it up and put it neatly back into its box. Selina watches me. I smile at her.

Selina's mother moves the roses from the centre of the table to a corner, 'so everyone can see each other,' she says. Clockwise round the table. Selina, her mother, her brother, his son, me, my mother, Selina's sister-in-law, my sister. There is an extra chair and place setting. My father's excuse: he is tired from gardening and needs to sleep. My mother, my sister and I glance over towards the wall as the sound of sport television suddenly filters through from next door. The volume is quickly turned low.

Sunday afternoon tea. Specially for Selina. The table has been laid with a white cloth and fine china. A big vase of roses. A huge cake. A large plate of biscuits. The serviettes have been folded on the diagonal.

There are small silver cake forks.

The cake is Selina's favourite. It is a cloud of meringue filled with strawberries. Home-made. Selina's mother serves. Selina is served first.

The weather is being talked about. It is humid. Sticky. Everyone feels sweaty. The imminent storm is discussed as the milk and sugar is passed back and forth across the table.

Selina just listens. She walks her fork up and down the serviette. She slides her fingers under her wig to scratch her head. She watches her nephew play his GameBoy. He notices her watching and begins to play with a fury. Pressing buttons like there is no tomorrow. His face a ball of anxiety. Showing off. He suddenly stops. He looks up at

Selina and slaps his forehead. He smiles. 'Me stupid, me died, me stupid, me di . . .' His voice trails off. He looks at his mother and then at Selina. There is an embarrassed silence around the table. Selina takes off her wig. She does it as if it were a crown, with both hands, and puts it down beside her plate. She surveys her audience. My mother asks Selina's mother how she manages to grow such beautiful roses.

Selina's nephew has slipped off his chair. He has crawled under the table.

I dream of Selina. It is our old school and she is standing at the end of a corridor silhouetted against a window. She is as I remember her at sixteen in the last months of her pregnancy, her hands resting on her full stomach. She seems peaceful, intent on whatever view she is holding through the window. The boys playing football is my guess from the sounds that are coming up from the playground. Her hair is all golden in the light. A soft halo around her head. She turns when she hears my footsteps. I see myself. It is me as I am now. I am pregnant, my swell as big, if not bigger, than Selina's. A grin spreads across my face. The dress I wear is tight and strains against the bulge. It rides up with each step I take. Almost up to my sex. I try to pull it down to cover my knees which makes Selina laugh. She holds her arms out to me and wraps them around me. She smells of pear drops. Our stomachs meet head on. Almost bounce. 'You really shouldn't be wearing such high heels in your condition,' she says. 'Cheeky,' I reply. That used to be my line to her. Except that she used to tut and tell me to shut up. We look at our feet. We are wearing the same shoes. I feel extreme pleasure; like the moment one leans back into a hot bath. The comfort and satisfaction of water against the body. Floating. Containment. Safety. 'Are you ready?' she asks. 'I'm ready,' I reply. 'Are you ready?' I ask. 'I'm ready,' she replies. We hold each other as close as we can. We count to ten. Our bodies fuse, merge into one. It brings an intense fever. It is this which wakes me.

I am late: there is no blood. There is only sick. Every morning. I do it quietly so my mother won't hear. Run the taps in the bath and the sink. I wait for seven days. Make it fourteen just to be sure.

She did it with both of them. Mr Jenson and Steve Baker. Both on the same day. Within the space of an hour. She didn't lie. She did do it behind the tree with Steve, like she said. Mr Jenson and her did it in the store cupboard. Up against the closed door, she said. She said she'd gone to him to tell him what had happened with Steve, and then he'd put his hand up her skirt. Mr Jenson did it to her while she was still wet with Steve.

'Did you want to?' I asked her.

'Always,' she said.

All the girls wanted to do it with Mr Jenson, she said. It was true. Even me. Even her mother. Who had. Even before Selina's father had died. Selina told me she caught them in the kitchen over the drying-up. His hand up her mother's skirt that time. Her hand between his legs rubbing and rubbing.

He promised Selina he wouldn't have sex with her mother again. He told her he loved her.

She was eight months pregnant when she caught them again. In the bedroom this time. Her mother sitting on his face. Wriggling. Making little dog whining noises. Their eyes were shut. They didn't see her. Selina closed the door quietly.

Later, as she and her mother watched a late-night film on

196

telly and her brother was flicking through the *NME* she said, 'Mr Jenson is in love with me.' And she told her mother everything.

If the baby was black like Steve she would be able to keep it. That is what her mother had said. The baby had been born white and had been taken away. But later, after Selina had signed adoption papers, the baby's skin had darkened. A nurse had told her this. Then it was too late. Not even the court could overturn the decision. Her mother cried for weeks and drank gin. She cried almost as much as Selina.

selina's child

She gives me the picture to look at.

It is a glossy photograph of a boy about ten years old. He has dark curly hair and brown eyes. His skin is coffee-coloured.

It is taken against a pale blue background. The sort that photographers use to suggest the sky. Mottled with white to give a sense of clouds and depth.

He is wearing a red V-neck sweater and a white shirt. He has both his elbows on the table and his chin in cupped in his hands. He is leaning slightly forward. He looks very happy. He is smiling, there is a gap between his top front teeth. On a white label on the back is typed his name: Jake. Underneath his name is the name of the school and the year. 1987.

The photograph arrived in a brown official-looking envelope, the ones with the window and a frank. With it came a compliment slip with the crest of the local council. On it was written 'As requested'. They had not written 'Do not bend' on the envelope. There is a light crease that runs diagonally down the photograph, across his ear and his hand. Selina tries to get rid of it by rubbing the back with her fingernail.

She hasn't shown anyone except me and her mother. She keeps it in a drawer by her bed next to her passport. She wants to get it covered in a special plastic so it won't fade.

my child

I am pregnant with Roberto's child.

It is a hot summer day. Selina and I are reclining under the shade of the big tree. Selina is lying. I am kneeling at her feet, my vest hiked up to my breasts, the fingers of both my hands splayed across the curve of my belly.

'So,' she says. Short and clipped. No smile on her face.

'So,' I say. I match her tone; hold back my smile.

'So . . .' she says again. More open this time, suggestive. She lowers her eyes to my stomach. Fixes her gaze.

I pull down my vest.

We are wearing matching vests and shorts. Hers in green. Mine in blue. I bought them specially. Her breasts have shrivelled to the size of ping-pong balls. I can see her ribs sticking through her vest. She wanted a tight vest. Even now, all skin and bones, she thinks it more sexy. She is playing with the tube at the point it goes into her chest. Scratching at it. With clean fingernails.

I pick a blade of grass and play with it. She could at least smile.

'What do you want, girl or boy?'

I smile at her.

'What do you want, girl or boy?'

She lifts her foot and climbs it over my stomach with her toes. It is tender. It is also a bribe.

'What do you want, girl or boy?'

She begins to push in with her heel. There is no promise behind the push.

I think I can hear the noise that she makes in her throat before she begins to cry.

I wrap my hands around her foot. I say: 'Girl.'

'Purl one, knit one, purl one, knit one.'

She reminds herself where she is.

The cancer is creeping through all her body and Selina knits.

She is making my baby a cardigan. She could never sew but she can knit. She has done the back and the sides and one arm. It will be for when it is first born. That is why she has done it in white. She has the tiny shapes laid out in front of her on the sheet on the bed. Nothing quite looks like it will fit together. As she has made it, the tension between the stitches has gone. She doesn't seem to notice. I don't say anything. It has taken her the two weeks she has been in bed to knit this much. She is quarterway through the second arm. She turns the needles round to begin a new row. I am watching her from the end of her bed. Without looking up, she says: 'What are you fucking staring at?'

'Nothing,' I say.

My days: I get up. I wash. My mother makes me breakfast. I go next door. At first, two days. Then four. Now six. I do not mind. I am glad to do it. To be at her disposal. To be with her. To go to the hospital with her for her weekly visits. I have passed on my work to colleagues. I have arranged an overdraft at the bank.

On the day I go home, water my plants, collect my post from the studio, she will ring me on my mobile. Order a magazine. A particular piece of fruit. A ball of white cotton.

We don't talk about it, the fact that she is dying, but it is there all the time between us. Like the ghost of her is already there. Waiting.

Yesterday Adele came to visit. Adele pretended nothing had changed. Perfect PR technique. Smiles had run between them like rickrack. She had brought the photographs of her wedding. Straight away, Selina said: 'Show me Roberto.'

She stole the picture of him. 'For Maddy,' she said. But she wanted to keep it. It is propped up against the lampstand on her bedside table.

I pick the picture up. Examine his features. Think about the miniature versions forming inside me. Turn the picture this way and that. Hope to get her attention. She continues to ignore me.

'So, you like the way he looks?' I say.

She puts down the needles. She takes the picture from me. She is about to speak, but her attention suddenly drifts. She whispers my name. She widens her eyes: her mother is coming up the stairs.

'Quick, quick,' she says. She pushes all the things towards me. A small smile on her face.

I scoop together the tiny shapes and the knitting needles and hide them under the sheet at the end of the bed. I sit on them. She hands me back the picture. I tuck it underneath my T-shirt; her face says she does not approve; it is too late to hide it somewhere else. Her mother has already walked through the door.

Our secret seems to raise the heat in the room. Her mother has brought Selina's liquid food. She puts it down on the bedside table. She fusses with the pillow behind Selina's head.

Selina and I try not to catch each other's eye. If we do, the giggles will be wild, high-pitched. Hysterical. We bite our lips.

'You're both very quiet,' she says; and she goes. Selina laughs first. We laugh until it hurts.

Selina has become afraid of the dark; the lights must be kept on throughout the night. She doesn't like the windows closed. They have taken her off the chemo. They have stopped all the radiation.

She sleeps nearly all the time. When she is awake she likes to watch television and she likes me to rub her feet. I am allowed to do this when she is awake and when she is asleep. There is nothing to talk about. Selina is not interested in anything any more. My baby's cardigan remains unfinished. It has been bundled into a brown paper bag and hidden under her bed.

From one day to the next her skin and the whites of her eyes turn pale yellow.

When she is awake and not watching television Selina is angry all of the time. She tells me and her mother to 'Fuck off'; she insists on going to the toilet alone. She shuffles like an old person across the landing and back. She leaves the door open. Her stomach is swollen. She wants to go but she can't; the laxatives don't work because of the painkillers. Her stomach is bigger than mine. This makes her smile. I think.

Another day. She forgets what she is saying. Her voice stops in mid-sentence. She wanted to play cards. She was telling me the rules of a card game. She stared into space searching for the words. She shook her head. She put down the cards. She lay down and hauled the sheets over her shoulders and slept.

Most of the time she sleeps. She sleeps with her face turned into the breeze. Her mother and I have conversations on the landing outside her bedroom. We whisper so she can't hear us. Her mother is saying it is best she goes back to hospital.

They have put her in a separate room. It is white, narrow and small. The window can't be opened. There is a picture of an autumn tree pasted on the wall opposite the bed.

Her dose of analgesics has been increased; her dose of tranquillisers has been increased. She feels nothing. She sleeps all the time. She no longer eats. She no longer gets out of bed.

She sleeps from morning till night. She sleeps all through the night. She sleeps day after day. She sleeps on her back. Her legs stretched out. She hardly moves at all. She has bedsores on her hips and her shoulders and her elbows.

She is beginning to smell: it is slightly sweet. Slightly rancid. Selina is rotting from the inside out.

The nurses change her sheets while she is still in the bed. They do it with practised ease. They rearrange the pillows. Fluff them up. They turn her from one side to the other. Once an hour. They show me and her mother how to feed her water with a sponge and then a mouth swab. The doctors take messages from her body. Her heartbeat rate. Her breath. They chart it on her graph. They increase the dosage of everything.

Adele and Jayne come to visit; they bring flowers. They stand at the end of her bed. They don't say very much; they don't stay very long.

In the basement of the hospital I am scanned. I watch the baby's heartbeat. I can see its tiny hands. I am given a black-

and-white picture. Upstairs I hold it up for Selina to see. Selina hasn't opened her eyes for days.

She has only been in hospital for three days.

Already there is the rattle in her breath.

Sometimes her face looks peaceful. Sometimes it looks agitated. I sit by her bed and hold her hand.

Next door in the visiting room family and friends are gathering. They are waiting. They drink brandy. They talk about things in the outside world.

It will be light soon. A doctor comes in. Takes Selina's pulse. Listens to Selina's chest. Smiles at me sympathetically. Leaves again. I hear him talking in the visiting room.

Suddenly her room is filling with people. They are taking their places around her bed.

I wait outside in the corridor.

Selina, Gabriel and I walk along the river bank. We walk up the hill to where the castle is and down again along the path that leads into the forest. We walk down the path three abreast, Gabriel in the middle to take care that his wings do not catch on any of the branches. Selina and I walk quietly, arms folded, eyes to the ground, watching our step, occasionally looking at each other and smiling. The forest path twists and turns. Around us the trees grow thick, thin out, grow thick again. Along the way Gabriel points out birds and animals. Eagle, squirrel, magpie, fox, jay.

At the darkest part of the forest there is always a breeze that makes all the branches creak like a hundred old doors being opened. We wait for it. Hear it gathering pace as it comes towards us, captures us, our hair blown across our faces, Gabriel's wings ruffled. And then it passes through beyond us, fades out into quietness, a few old twigs falling into the undergrowth.

Gabriel takes our hands. 'Close your eyes,' he says, and Selina and I close our eyes, but continue walking, led by him. We know to stay silent.

After a while, he says: 'See how the darkness is no longer a place of danger but of infinite possibility.'

In the darkness, our every sensation becomes more pronounced. The touch of his skin against ours and the breeze against our faces, the sound of each footstep, the papery flap of a bird's wing, the buzz of an insect, the hush of the moving leaves in the wind. The whole world seems to rush in and fill our blood with the promise of good things.

'I want this moment to last for ever,' Selina whispers.

'So do I,' I whisper back.

Gabriel very gently squeezes our hands.

'Ssh . . . you'll spoil it,' he says.

He makes us stand still a while, eyes still closed. Focuses us on a bird call, a magpie's caw, or the mew of an eagle, and then, when he feels we are quiet enough again, leads us on. Our eyes still closed.

When he tells us to open our eyes we walk in silence but eagerly towards the pool of sun at the end of the path where the trees open out into a clearing. There are tall yellow flowers growing here, and a small pond, long grass, a lone apple tree. Here we lie and sunbathe. Selina plays with my hair, humming gently. We eat some apples and chit-chatter softly about nothing in particular, as friends do. Gabriel has to lie on his stomach on account of his wings, which he keeps high and tight together so that the sun can get to his shoulders. He falls asleep. He snores. Small snores that make Selina and me giggle. We lie on our backs and watch the sky.

'I'm going to go soon,' I say.

'I know,' says Selina.

'Gabriel will look after you.'

'I know,' says Selina.

'Is that all you can say?'

She rolls over on to her side.

'What do you want me to say?'

I roll over on to my side so I face her.

211

'I don't know.'

Selina raises her eyebrows. We stare at each other for a little while and then we roll over on to our backs again and watch the sky. It is very blue but seems thin and fragile. There seems to be no distance between us and it. Nothing at all. As if we could reach our hands up and push them straight through into the black and stars beyond.

a note on the author

Janni Visman was born in 1960, and studied film at the London College of Printing and mixed media at The Slade School of Fine Art. She lives in London.

a note on the type

The text of this book is set in Linotype Sabon, named after the type founder, Jacques Sabon. It was designed by Jan Tschichold and jointly developed by Linotype, Monotype and Stempel, in response to a need for a typeface to be available in identical form for mechanical hot metal composition and hand composition using foundry type.

Tschichold based his design for Sabon roman on a fount engraved by Garamond, and Sabon italic on a fount by Granjon. It was first used in 1966 and has proved an enduring modern classic.